FRACTURED POWER

FRACTURED POWER
CHOSEN BY FREYA™
BOOK FOUR

MICHAEL ANDERLE

DISRUPTIVE IMAGINATION

DON'T MISS OUR NEW RELEASES

Join the LMBPN email list to be notified of new releases and special promotions (which happen often) by following this link:

http://lmbpn.com/email/

This book is a work of fiction. All of the characters, organizations, and events portrayed in this novel are either products of the author's imagination or are used fictitiously. Sometimes both.

Copyright © 2023 LMBPN Publishing
Cover Art by Jake @ J Caleb Design
http://jcalebdesign.com / jcalebdesign@gmail.com
Cover copyright © LMBPN Publishing
A Michael Anderle Production

LMBPN Publishing supports the right to free expression and the value of copyright. The purpose of copyright is to encourage writers and artists to produce the creative works that enrich our culture.

The distribution of this book without permission is a theft of the author's intellectual property. If you would like permission to use material from the book (other than for review purposes), please contact support@lmbpn.com. Thank you for your support of the author's rights.

LMBPN® Publishing
2375 E. Tropicana Avenue, Suite 8-305
Las Vegas, Nevada 89119 USA

Version 1.00, December 2023
eBook ISBN: 979-8-88878-710-6
Print ISBN: 979-8-88878-711-3

THE FRACTURED POWER TEAM

Thanks to the JIT Readers
Dave Hicks
Dorothy Lloyd
Christopher Gilliard
John Ashmore
Diane L. Smith
Jackey Hankard-Brodie
Jan Hunnicutt

Editor
The SkyFyre Editing Team

CHAPTER ONE

Barrow Company Dig Site 106, Gotland Island, Sweden, Tuesday Afternoon

Terra Olsen could not believe how much her life had changed in the last year.

She had discovered multiple artifacts belonging to a goddess that granted her super strength, teleportation, and the ability to weave *seidr* into balls of fire, shields of energy, and a few other more interesting, if less consistent, tricks. Even more exciting, she no longer worked for an insurance company and was instead an *actual* archeologist.

Not only an archeologist, but one working on Gotland Island, home of the Spillings hoard, the largest find of Viking silver treasure ever discovered. If Harris Barrow's hunch was correct, Terra might soon unearth something even more important than a cache of silver coins from all over the ancient world.

The crowning object might have to stay secret, but Terra would not let it get her down. They had already discovered so much here. Every day was an adventure, and Terra didn't mind that this particular adventure did not involve people shooting at her.

Merely walking through the cave felt like entering a dream. Stalactites and stalagmites, still growing but hardly changed since this place was first used to stash treasure, lined the path of thick mats they'd placed through the cave. Water had carved the main passage, but not all at once. Instead, it had paused and formed larger rooms, then smaller ones, separating and rejoining as the cave went deeper and deeper. Here and there, active flows grew crystals before their eyes while other sections seemed frozen in time.

She wondered what the Vikings thought of this place when they had first discovered it. Did they believe it was an entrance to another world? That the thirsty roots of the world tree had made it? Did they find beauty in the formations, or were caves more a part of their world than they were a part of Terra's?

For Vikings who had spent days or weeks at sea, a cave like this might represent a respite from the ravages of the natural world. A place to warm up or cool down, depending on the season. A place that was dry compared to the outside world.

It was different for Terra, who had grown up in the modern world of air conditioning and affordable roofing solutions.

Maybe the Vikings viewed this place as a step outside their normal existence, as Terra did. That might have been why they used it to store so much treasure.

"Oh, look. Another dirham." Leif tossed the ancient silver coin over his shoulder as if it were nothing more than an American penny.

"Don't do that!" Terra scrambled after the coin. She picked it up in a gloved hand, placed it in a plastic bag, and marked it with its relative location. "That could have come all the way from Egypt or even farther!"

Countless objects like the coin lay scattered throughout the cave they were exploring. Caves riddled the limestone beneath Gotland. Lummelundagrottan was the most famous and a regular stop for tourists. However, it held few artifacts besides detritus from the various mills built over the centuries to use the same water that carved the cave.

Their cave was smaller and located in the back of a farm. Barrow had become involved in it because there had been a small shrine to Freya on the farm. The farmer had thought it was only an interesting piece of architecture until a recent storm had opened a sinkhole filled with all sorts of things.

Some of it must have washed there from the storm, but deposits of coins and a few bars of silver seemed to indicate the cave had been used to store valuable artifacts.

The locals had thought it was a stroke of luck that the rains had opened the entrance to the sinkhole, but Terra had other suspicions. The last time they had spoken, the goddess Freya told her she would not intervene with Terra's quest on Midgard. However, she was beginning to think the gods of Asgard might not be the most honest of beings in the nine realms.

"Big deal," Leif muttered sarcastically. "The Vikings who worshipped my great-grandmother went farther afield than Egypt. We're here for another of Freya's vestments, not the trinkets they brought back."

"If you could tell us precisely *where* that vestment is, or even what it is, we could skip ahead to that part."

"I would like to do that, but it's not so simple. Look here." He held up a rolled piece of leather. "Since you, let's say, reinvigorated me with *seidr*, I've been able to feel the flow of it better than I could before. I've managed to make this map."

Terra smiled as inky marks appeared on the piece of supple leather. It looked like an unseen paintbrush was swiping across the brown surface with ink and water, leaving behind a map of Northern Europe centered on Scandinavia. Norway, Sweden, and Denmark surrounded by the Northern and Baltic Seas. Terra made out a corner of the UK and the northern shore of Poland and Germany.

Leif moved his fingers across the leather, a gesture that would have looked the same on a touchscreen. The map centered on Gotland Island, which was off the southeastern coast of Sweden. On the other side of the Baltic Sea lay Lithuania, Latvia, and Estonia, then Finland to the north. Saint Petersburg was slightly too far east to be visible at this magnification.

"You can see how Gotland is more reddish than the rest?"

"I can." Terra marveled at how the countries' shorelines seemed to redraw themselves with an unseen pen occasionally.

"That's because *seidr* is stronger here. I can *feel* that, but when I zoom in?" Leif expanded the map until the island filled the entire piece of leather. "It won't go any closer. I can sense it near here, but that's it. It could be in a lake, for all I know. Or under a shop. Perhaps one of those with a bag of Bilar? Who would have thought to make a sweet out of a carriage?" The Asgardian's stomach rumbled at the thought of another helping of cheap candy.

"Well, if your internal magic GPS can only get us within a hundred kilometers, we'll have to do the rest of it the old-fashioned way. That means documenting everything we find."

"I have been documenting everything. Observe." Leif zoomed in closer with a flourish, and a map of the cave appeared, like pools of ink flowing into each other. "If there's some pattern to the cave, I don't see it. It looks random to me. I also haven't seen any places that scream *hidden* room."

"It's impressive, but I don't see any marks for the artifacts we've found. You should at least add the coins. They're from another continent! How is that not amazing? Everyone thinks the modern world is the pinnacle of a global economy, but these prove trade has been going on at a continental scale for centuries."

"We're on an island. Isn't everything here from another continent?" Leif protested.

"Oh, cheer up. If it weren't for you, we'd be digging in an entirely different city. We'll probably find the artifacts *years* sooner, thanks to you!"

Leif groaned. "Being immortal does not mean I don't get bored, you know. Maybe it *is* in a lake. We should check and maybe use the chance to try out your underwater breathing again."

"The last time we tried that, it took me an hour before I could breathe air again. I'm not in any mood to repeat it."

Leif chuckled as if her gasping for air like a fish on a hook was anything besides terrifying. "I'm sure you'll get it in less time. Maybe fifteen minutes?"

"Even if I did want to try my luck at being a mermaid in a mountain lake, which I *don't*, by the way, this dig is hardly going to progress if we're not here. We're understaffed. Basically uninsurable."

Leif snorted. "Good to know your former profession of notarized gambler is still in your heart, Terra. And the diggers we hired are doing fine. I checked in on them this morning, and they found a hammer or a shovel or something in one of the caves deeper down."

"A shovel? Why didn't you tell me?"

"Because…it's a shovel? Freya is the mistress of many things, but digging holes is not one of them. We could expect to find another piece of jewelry or perhaps some part of her chariot that she left here. Although the last time we saw her, the chariot seemed to work fine. Oh, maybe it's a cat toy!"

Terra wasn't listening. She was already heading deeper into the cave system toward where the current excavation was happening. One advantage of working in a cave instead of digging directly through the ground was less excavation. Instead of sorting through layers and layers of soil and documenting every shard of metal and sometimes even the pollen, they could continue through the stone tunnels of the cave system until they reached a blockade.

They'd placed most of what they found in various alcoves throughout the cave. Already, they had discovered various coins, goblets, rings, silver ingots, and a handful of gems. They had done some mild excavation here and there to ensure soil hadn't filled in the cave ground, but everything had been stone. The cave existed before the Vikings found it, and they had not altered it.

So far, anyway.

A shovel could indicate the Vikings who had discovered this place, or more likely taken control of it from the people who had been here from before they arrived, had made some improvements of their own. Like, say, a room with an anachronistic sculpture of Freya that held a sliver of the goddess.

"I don't think she dug herself a shrine down there if that's what you're thinking." Leif made an effort to keep up with Terra. "To be honest, I don't know who made any of these shrines. Humans, I suppose, but then you would think someone would remember being called into work by the goddess of beauty."

"I think it's safe to assume their existence is lost to time. If someone knew about them, we would have been confronted by now," Terra mentioned.

"That would be troublesome, wouldn't it? Can you imagine? Some hapless mortal thinking they have a claim to a sliver of my great-grandmother's power simply because she gave their ancestor a job?"

"That would be better than someone randomly finding them. I'm glad we're not competing with Villon anymore, but any of our artifacts would be dangerous if they fell into the wrong hands. People cause all sorts of damage through simple ignorance, and that's without superhuman power."

Leif nodded. "Mortals do have their shortcomings, it's true."

"Sir?" It was one of the diggers from the room ahead of them. "Did you say mortals, sir?"

"Marbles," Terra blurted. "Marbles have their shortcomings."

"Ma'am?" The digger looked from Terra to Leif, obviously confused.

"Some archeologists use marbles to, uh… find the deepest part of the cave. They let them roll right down there. Yup. I don't think it's the best method, though. Doesn't take into account if a part of the cave goes uphill."

"Right," The digger replied in Swedish-accented English. "Did you come to see the shovel? I had expected you to come sooner."

"Yes, the shovel!" Terra exclaimed, desperate to steer the conversation better than her imagined marble theory.

"It is here." He handed her a bag with a banged-up piece of rusty iron inside. It looked more like a horseshoe than a shovel.

"Oh wow, fascinating!" Terra took the bag gingerly, not wanting it to fall apart. It didn't bear much resemblance to modern, steel-pressed shovels.

"It looks like a mouth guard for a giant," Leif remarked. He seemed more impressed by the flavors that chips came in than he was by the priceless artifact.

Terra gave him a *shush* look, but the digger only chuckled. This was the land of the giants, after all. He probably thought Leif was joking around.

"Most of their shovels were wood, actually," Terra explained to Leif. "They wrapped this iron bit around the wooden part because it was stronger, but they didn't want to waste metal on something like this. Better to use it for a weapon."

Leif shrugged. "I'm glad I was a librarian and never a digger in Midgard."

"Excuse me?" the digger who was most certainly from Midgard asked. Then shouts came from deeper in the cave, which saved Leif from explaining what he meant by that.

Terra tried to stay calm as the sound of footsteps approaching echoed through the cave. She wanted to rush in, to help, but she knew the biggest risk was a cave-in. Her running down wouldn't help with that. She had already been trapped in a cave once and didn't want to risk it again. However, now that she could teleport, it was less of a risk.

She was not prepared for the word she heard echoing up the tunnels.

"*Orm! Orm!*"

"Did I hear that right? Are they saying..."

"Snake." Leif polished his glasses that never needed polishing. Bygul's eye twinkled on the end of the chain that hung from his spectacles.

He wasn't the only one packing an artifact with *seidr* inside. Terra wore Freya's bracers underneath her jacket. The cool weather outside justified the wardrobe choice, and while most people removed their outer layer in the relative warmth of the cave, it wasn't unusual to leave hers on. She hadn't been expecting to fight a serpent, though.

The only one she knew of from Norse legend was too big to fit in a cave, even one as deep as this.

She had started to feel almost silly, wearing the bracers day after day when nothing ever happened to justify the magic power they granted her, but she could not take them off. She enjoyed archeology, but part of her wanted to use the *seidr* she controlled. She wanted to fight, to brawl, to challenge others in battle, and to come out victorious. It was a new sensation for her, but she could not help but like it. So when Leif confirmed the people were yelling *snake*, Terra's heartbeat quickened in anticipation, not fear.

Three diggers ran past, followed by their local expert, Per Bengtsson.

"I cannot work with these people," he exclaimed, polishing his glasses as he approached. Unlike Leif's glasses, Per's were perpetually dirty. He had not complained yet to the Asgardian, but Terra thought she saw him glance at Leif's sparkly lenses more than once.

"They were yelling about a snake?" Terra asked.

"They are superstitious children!" Per replied. "I told your employer we needed *professionals*. Archeology is not unheard of on this island. We have many people who would not run at the first shadow they see."

"I understand, but we've talked about this. After the media circus surrounding the Spillings hoard, my employer wanted to maintain a low profile. If we hired every expert on the island, we'd have already attracted every camera crew. We had to pick the best of the best, which is why you're here, Dr. Bengtsson."

Bengtsson shrugged at that and smiled. He had a bit of a temper, but playing to his ego almost always soothed the man. "I suppose I understand. Though if everyone goes running every time something odd happens, it will create the same circus you fear, will it not?"

"If something has spooked the crew, maybe we can swap stories over a bottle of *akvavit* later, mm?" Leif asked.

If playing to his pride didn't work, promising the archeologist a drink of the vile herbed liquor he liked so much always did. Power of Freya or not, Terra could not stand the stuff, but Leif seemed to like it. Probably because he had no taste and thought candy was a delicacy.

"I'm always pleased to talk about the day's work with you, Mr. Freyason," Bengtsson stated. "We can add a bit more to your map?"

"That would be a pleasure, yes," Leif returned.

"You showed him your map?" Terra asked through gritted teeth.

"Of course!" Leif pulled the piece of leather back out and unraveled it. Where before the lines seemed to be rewriting themselves constantly, now it was still. It showed the cave system and nothing more. "Maybe we can add the locations of those coins we've found."

"I've been telling you!" Bengtsson looked inordinately pleased to have someone doing what he had already told him to do. "Perhaps a shower first, though? Maybe a sauna? It is moist in the lower levels."

Bengtsson was filthy, as were all the diggers who had fled past them.

"There's no threat down there, then?" Terra asked.

"No threat whatsoever." Bengtsson snorted. Terra got the feeling if she had not been his boss, he might have patted her on the head. "There was a channel of running water underneath some thick clay. It began to glow, which made it appear to move in the low light. These superstitious locals saw that and claimed the impossible. Nothing to concern yourself over."

She might have believed him if it were not for the impossibly loud hissing she heard from deeper in the cave.

CHAPTER TWO

Barrow Company Dig Site 106, Gotland Island, Sweden, Tuesday Afternoon

"That's running water, then?" Terra asked Bengtsson, but he was already gone, moving up a passage and waving farewell to them.

"Superstitions! All superstitions!" He must have thought Terra had turned around before he made the shape of a rune with his hand.

"Come on," Terra told Leif. There was a time when she would have dismissed all of it, but that time was long past.

"Are you certain?" Leif fiddled with Bygul's eye on his glasses chain. "Are snakes not common in Sweden? I believe they used to ravage much of Midgard, at least to hear Thor tell it. And you are without Freya's ax."

"We'll be all right. There are some snakes here, but none count as 'giant.' I don't really want to see an adder, though. Their bites are supposed to be painful."

"How painful?" Leif asked, following her at a distance.

"Leif! Are you afraid of snakes? I would think a man

who faced down gunfire and the magic wand of the god of chaos wouldn't be bothered by a little slithering."

"You try growing up being told bedtime stories about the Midgard Serpent. If that thing so much as opens its mouth to stop biting its own tail, Ragnarök was supposed to begin."

"What do you mean *was* supposed to begin?" Terra asked as they entered the furthest excavated room at the end of the cave. As Bengtsson had said, it was quite muddy, and steam ran along one of the walls. Only a single lamp remained lit, knocked on its side. Terra placed a hand on a wall and followed it as she headed for a pile of tools and flashlights. "Isn't Ragnarök supposed to be coming? Odin talked that way, too. He said you earned a place at the *next* Ragnarök. Oh, would you look at those freaky legs!"

Without noticing it, she had touched the legs of a spider as big as her face resting on the cave wall. It was black and brown, though one of its legs had a glint of gold. It scuttled when she touched it, which totally freaked her out. So she did what anyone who hated spiders would do when confronted with one big enough to eat them if they had super-human strength. She tried to squash it to nothing.

Her fist slammed into the spider and went through it, then through the stone wall of the cave behind it. The wall shattered, and dust and mud came down from the ceiling.

Terra leaped backward, putting herself between the falling debris and Leif. As long as she could touch him, she could teleport them out of here if this became a full-blown collapse. But the wall held after the initial fall of debris.

"Is it not enough to smash a spider? You must obliterate it?" He was laughing, though.

"I guess I don't know my own strength," Terra replied. It was true. Sort of. Or it would have been if she hadn't been training with Leif for months.

"I may not like snakes, but it seems Freya chose someone frightened of spiders!"

"I'm not frightened of them. They're weird, is all. Haven't you seen the way they move?" Terra shuddered.

"I barely got an opportunity before you sent that one to Muspelheim!"

"You know, you're talking pretty tough for a guy worried about being bitten by a snake. Spiders are venomous, too. Some of them are deadlier than snakes."

Terra didn't know if that was true, but she wouldn't have Leif teasing her about this until the end of the world.

"Oh, I'm quite aware. I saw a film about them recently. Freaks with Eight Legs, it was called. Or Eight Freaky Legs. Something like that. Quite enjoyable, I assure you. Though the spider you saw was a bit smaller than the ones besotting that poor town."

"You know those were computer-generated, right?"

"Terra, behind you!"

"Don't change the subject," Terra stated. "You keep getting duped by effects. We're good at faking in movies. It's one of the modern wonders of the world. You don't need to be embarrassed. I thought it was cute that you cried when ET phoned home."

"I'm not embarrassed about embracing my emotions, but you're about to be if you don't turn around and see what you have done."

"I know what I did. I squashed the hell out of that spider." Terra turned anyway, ready to see nothing and for

Leif to laugh. In a way, she saw exactly that. Where the wall had been was now nothing. No dust, no mud. No more limestone behind the fallen sheets.

Instead, there was an empty passageway.

"My spider sense is tingling," Terra muttered. She picked up an electric lamp, turned it on, then gestured for Leif to follow her into the passage.

She paused at the entryway, looking at the edge of the tunnel. It seemed natural enough, except for the lip, which appeared built up from layers of mud. She could even see fingerprints. She couldn't help but grin. Those could be the fingerprints of Vikings from over a thousand years ago!

"I don't think this is merely another passageway," she commented to Leif.

"I think you're right about that." Leif's eyes widened with wonder.

The farthest shafts of light from the lamp barely reached the room at the end of the passage. Terra found that she could not speak. The room had taken her breath away.

A statue of Freya stood in the center, slightly larger than life. One arm was outstretched and pointing up and ahead while the other hung at her side. Her flowing robe hid almost nothing of her god-like anatomy beneath. That effect alone, the way the sculptor had made the marble look like transparent fabric, would have been breathtaking, but it wasn't that article of clothing drawing the eye.

Freya wore a cloak made of feathers. Terra approached, trying to wrap her head around how long it must have taken to carve such a garment. Each feather was crafted with painstaking precision, detailing not only the central shaft of each feather but every individual barb. The feathers gently curled toward the ends, except it looked as if the wind had disheveled a few barbs.

It wasn't only the detail of the garment that amazed Terra, though. It was also how it all flowed over Freya's shoulders, around her neck, and down her back to accentuate her beauty, strength, and fearlessness. It was a masterpiece. A glorious piece of art that could hardly have been created by a modern artist with unlimited time and funds, let alone a Viking from a millennia past. The Vikings were many things, but they were not known for their artistic skills.

Yet this one was a masterwork, lost in a cave in the back of a farm for who knew how long.

It wasn't the only masterpiece in the room. Behind the statue of Freya, on the cave wall, was a mosaic of startling beauty. It depicted a sky filled with hawks, falcons, eagles, and other birds of prey. Some were made of hundreds of pieces of stone and glass. Others, smaller and in the apparent distance, were a few perfectly cut pieces arranged to create the suggestion of a bird that was somehow more moving and poignant than the larger, more realistic ones.

"I guess we know what's in there, then." Leif pointed at the statue.

Terra had not noticed the elaborately carved box in one of the statue's hands. The arm at her side was not resting but holding tight to the true prize of the room.

"Well, at least it's not hidden," Terra remarked. "I wouldn't want to do anything to damage this room. It's unbelievable." She stepped toward the box at Freya's side.

"Then stop where you are."

Terra turned to see a man standing at the entrance to the room they had come through. He was devilishly good-looking and dressed immaculately in a color scheme Terra could hardly wrap her head around.

He wore purple slacks and a purple jacket over a white shirt. The ascot at his neck shimmered silver in the shifting light of Terra's lamp. A purple hat with a rather dashing brim sported a silver hat band that perfectly matched the ascot. His fingers glittered with large, tacky rings. Mostly gold, though some bore stones. His belt was black leather with a silver buckle that matched his shoes.

His shoes bothered Terra the most. They looked more suited for a dance floor than an archeological dig.

"He's completely clean," Leif hissed. "Not a speck of mud on him."

It was true.

Unlike Terra, Leif, Bengtsson, and every other digger in their employ, none of the clay-like mud that filled the limestone cave clung to his clothes. Not even the bottom cuff of his purple pants was smudged. It was as if he'd appeared in the hall out of thin air.

"Who are you, and what are you doing on my dig?" Terra asked, trying to keep her voice level. She wanted to show neither fear nor anger, not yet.

"My name is Marcus. A pleasure." He removed his hat to reveal slicked-back black hair, combed perfectly despite being stuck under the hat. "I am here for the same reason as you. I am interested in antiquities. Though I would not dare claim such a beautiful sculpture could belong to *anyone.*"

He took a few steps closer and put his hands on his hips

as he gazed up at the stern yet beautiful face of the goddess Freya. "A wonder, is it not? And to think, no puzzle I can detect. Maybe finding the room was supposed to be the challenge."

"This property is under the jurisdiction of the Barrow company. While everything we find here will belong to the Swedish government, you are currently trespassing on *our* site. We are authorized to use force if you do not comply." Terra made her voice like iron.

"Oh, I noticed you are not one to shy away from force. That spider really was in a lucky spot, was it not? Without it, you might have collapsed the entire cavern instead of revealing this room. You owe it thanks, I would say."

"You need to go," Terra stated. Maybe that was blunt enough.

"Fair enough, and I will, as soon as I get what I came for." Marcus took another step toward the statue and quirked his head to the side. "I don't detect a puzzle, do you? The box is in the open, which surely means we can take it and figure out how to open it later. Would you agree?"

He reached out to take the container but was unable to. Terra had grabbed him by the wrist. She was surprised at how pleasurable she found it to get mud on his purple suit.

"Either you do not know who you are dealing with, which makes you a fool, or you know exactly who she is, which makes you a potential enemy," Leif remarked.

"More than potential, really." Marcus winked, but when his eyelid opened back up, it faded completely. His nose sunk into his face, and his hat slid back on his head, becoming a hood. The wrist that Terra gripped became thinner and pulled backward into his body. His other arm vanished as well, while his legs came together to become one long, sinuous rope of muscle, twisted and coiled around itself.

Its back was dark, nearly black, though considering the low light, it could have been a rich purple. A more subtle version of the clothing he had worn. A single gold band circled the serpent's tail. He grinned. The last human part of him was his mouth, but he had fangs instead of human teeth and a forked tongue.

"I will ask you once more to give me the bracers." The snake hissed, his forked tongue flicking in and out.

Leif sighed. "You know, I think I would have preferred it if the workers were jumping at shadows."

Then the snake attacked.

CHAPTER THREE

Barrow Company Dig Site 106, Gotland Island, Sweden, Tuesday Afternoon

The serpent uncoiled like a spring at Terra and tried to sink its fangs into her chest.

Terra sidestepped, barely getting clear. Then she threw a punch with such force that the snake's head hit the ground, and the cave rumbled. The force of the blow moved along its body like a Slinky toy before the tip of its tail quivered. It shook its head from the blow.

"Had enough?" Terra asked. Her practice had been paying off.

"Hardly," Marcus hissed, then whipped his tail and took her legs out from under her.

She crashed to the ground but scrambled back to her feet. The snake had coiled the tip of its tail around Leif's midsection and was drawing the Asgardian closer.

"That is quite enough! The purple proved you were not from this realm, but trying to eat me instead of the wonderful confectioneries they have here is too much!" Leif shouted at the snake.

Terra pointed her fists at the snake and blasted a fireball at it. It slammed into the snake, and Terra thought victory was hers until the ball puffed off its skin into smoke.

It hardly damaged the creature, but it had distracted it from trying to swallow Leif. It let him go, knocking a coil into him that sent him sprawling against the gorgeous mosaic. Then, it slithered toward her, pumping its huge coils back and forth with dizzying speed.

Terra shot darts of white-hot energy at its face that swirled and twisted before striking it. The snake hissed and ducked, folding its hood around its eyes. That was something, but not exactly the success Terra had been hoping for.

A huge house cat joined the fray, leaping for the disoriented snake, but with a swipe of its tail, the illusion Leif had created puffed into nothing.

"Our abilities are weak against him when he's in this form! It must be the magic he's using. It gives him natural shielding!" Leif exclaimed.

Terra didn't think anything was natural about a man with odd fashion choices shape-shifting into a snake, but now was not the time to discuss linguistic drift across the centuries or between the realms. Instead, she braced herself, pointed her hands at the snake, and blasted more darts.

Marcus, if he was still in control of this body, came for the bait. He slithered toward her, not bothering to block the darts with his hood. He thought it was his natural shielding, but Terra had taken all of the heat out of them. They were only motes of light now, which used much less *seidr*.

It let her conserve as much as she could for when he lunged.

She didn't have to wait long. After he got his coils beneath him, Marcus lunged at her.

Terra was ready.

She leaned backward enough to let the snake's fangs miss her. She grabbed his jaw, one hand between the two long fangs at the bottom and the other between the top two. She was inches from the snake's eye, which was wide and slitted, though Terra could not tell by the reptilian features if he was scared. His tongue flicked back and forth, touching Terra's face.

It was gross, but not as gross as what she was about to do to him.

With one hand on each of his jaws and the power of Freya strengthening her, Terra pulled. Immediately, she felt the snake's strength as he tried to resist her, but a snake was not a crocodile nor a hyena. Its strength was not in its ability to snap its jaws closed. Terra leveraged the jaws farther apart. She felt something snap and knew Marcus had unhinged a jaw in an attempt to save himself.

His sinuous body thrashed against her, trying to disrupt her or knock her off balance, but the reptile had no real plan. However, Terra knew she only needed to pull the jaws apart. She felt another snap and understood no bones were stopping her now, only sinew. The fight was over, and the snake knew it.

That must have been why he changed shape. Not into a

man, but into a wasp. A large wasp, but still small enough to slip through her fingers.

Terra shot darts of energy after the wasp. Most missed, but one hit directly. It knocked the wasp from the air, but that didn't seem to bother Marcus much. He was already transforming into a bighorn sheep. He kicked up on his hind legs, pawing at the air, then dropped his head and front legs and charged.

Terra dodged and tried to grab the sheep in a headlock but only succeeded in knocking him along. He crashed into a wall, and the cave around them rumbled.

"Maybe not the best time to get into a fight of brute strength," Leif mused from the far side of the room.

"I can't zap him. I can't punch him. What am I supposed to do?"

Marcus shifted into his human form in the blink of an eye. One moment, the sheep was there, digging at the ground with hooves like iron. The next, he walked out of the animal, and it ceased to be.

"Obviously, you are supposed to surrender the box and its contents to the superior man."

"Let me know if you see anyone who fits that description." Terra blasted a fireball at Marcus. Leif must have been right about the shifted form providing him protection because Marcus was unwilling to let the fireball strike him. Instead, he became a black bear. The fireball crashed into the bear's hairy chest, but it hardly singed the hair, let alone damage the skin beneath.

Marcus the bear tromped toward her on his hind legs, swinging paws big as baseball gloves and tipped with claws.

She caught one blow on her bracers and moved backward, putting the sculpture between her and her opponent.

Marcus roared and shuffled around the statue. Another bear appeared to challenge him, but he swiped the illusion, immediately recognizing it for what it was.

"I'm afraid my specific strengths are poorly suited to this battle," Leif lamented, sidelined with his magic spectacles.

"I'd be more than happy to accept some strategic input." Terra leaped forward and caught the bear's face with an elbow. He flew and hit the mosaic, knocking a few beautiful pieces of stone away.

Terra gasped at the desecration.

The bear only roared, then it was Marcus again, laughing. "You do understand I can become a bug, correct? If you bring this entire place down, I'll crawl out. How did you think I got in here in the first place?"

Then he was a lion, leaping at them. Terra caught his huge bulk on her chest and tried to toss him overhead, but that would have crashed him into the statue of Freya. Instead of letting go, she held on, and they tumbled into a pile.

Perhaps a good old-fashioned wrestling match would favor her. She wrapped the lion's head in one of her arms and squeezed, but as soon as she did, Marcus was a lion no longer. A rat scurried from her grip onto her back, then an orangutan choked her from behind.

She stumbled with the monkey on her back and crashed him into a wall.

"Terra, I'd rather not go back to the scenario in which

we first met!" Leif shouted as dust fell from the roof of the cavern.

Marcus had already changed again. A gecko scrambled over the cave ceiling. Terra blasted it with darts, but she couldn't hit it. Not even hard enough to make it shed its skin. Instead, Marcus became a bat and flew at her face. When he struck, he wasn't a bat but a wolverine. It thrashed and slashed at her face as she threw it off.

"What about the ax? This magic can't stop the ax, right?" Terra suggested to Leif.

"I wouldn't think so. The ax is supposed to be the master of *seidr*. He shouldn't be able to use magic to resist it."

"Great. You think you can hold him? I'll be right back."

"I would love to," Leif replied. Another copy of him stepped from his chest, then a third and a fourth.

The wolverine snarled and slashed the legs of the original. Only he was no longer an illusion.

"Oh, so you can't see through an illusion. You simply know better than to let an animal bother you," Leif observed from six different bodies at once.

The wolverine snarled and transformed into a tiger. It lashed its tail as it growled at one version of Leif, then swiped at another, turning it into a puff of smoke.

Terra saw nothing more of their battle before she teleported back to the surface.

She appeared in a cavern slightly underground. It was near the cave entrance, and the team had gone through it repeatedly before Terra finally declared it finished and deemed it off-limits. She had done that in the anticipation of needing a moment like this.

She could teleport without being able to see where she was going, but it was risky. She had spent plenty of time in this room, memorizing every single stalactite, stalagmite, and column to prepare for teleporting here and not appearing halfway through a stone feature. She reappeared an inch above the ground and dropped, landing with a reassuring *thump* of her boots.

Yet she had no time to celebrate a job well done. She had stashed the ax in her car, and she needed it now. She ran out of the cave, hoping the diggers had all decided to go home early, but of course, they hadn't. No one wanted to abandon work early in this economy. They were milling around, waiting for the end of the work day, chatting among themselves.

"Oh my god, I can't believe I forgot my digital camera!" Terra shouted as she sprinted past them toward her car.

She reached it in less than a minute, which was still too long. She popped the trunk and grabbed her bag of "camera equipment." The bag was worn and beaten, and she had planned it that way. The hope was if some random thief found it, they'd skip it for the much nicer-looking camera bag she'd crammed with valuables as bait. The ax inside didn't look fancy, but it held the power of a goddess.

She ran back toward the cave with her dirty, weathered bag.

"What about your camera equipment?" Bengtsson asked.

"Turns out I only need batteries!" she shouted as she ran past the crew. "Oh, go ahead and call it a day! We'll finish up and see you tomorrow. No need to clock out. We'll cover it!"

Then she vanished inside the cave. She went to the room she had appeared in and tried to catch her breath. She had teleported here a dozen times but had never teleported into the room with Freya's statue. She'd never seen it before today.

Could she teleport down there safely? If she was off by so much as a foot, she could end up inside a wall. But no, she could visualize the room. It was nothing if not memorable.

She pictured herself standing in front of the larger-than-life statue of Freya. She imagined her outstretched arm, the cloak of feathers on her back, the box in her other hand. She imagined the mosaic behind her, remembering how many paces it had taken to walk around the statue. She felt like she had the room in her head. It was time to teleport.

Only after she called *seidr* into her did she realize she might aim it to land where Leif or Marcus stood.

"Oh, for the love of the old gods!" Marcus cursed when Terra reappeared in front of the talking lion.

He rolled out of the way, and Terra turned to face him.

"Terra, I was hoping I'd see you." Leif's shirt was torn to shreds, and he had bloody gashes across his chest and one arm. He also had a massive bruise on one eye, and his nose looked broken. "You'd think the lion would be the worst, and you'd be wrong. You do not want to tangle with the gorilla."

Marcus only laughed. "You came back here with a sack? What are you going to do, put me inside it?"

Terra reached inside and pulled out Freya's ax. It was a simple weapon. Not worked over in gold runes like the bracers or a creation of delicate beauty like Brísingamen. It was a wooden shaft with a piece of iron wrapped around the end, hammered to flare into a blade on one side. It was not even big enough to warrant the use of two hands. Yet there was something *more* to the weapon. Terra felt the power inside it and its thirst for more.

Marcus was not oblivious to the power she held in the palm of her hand. He growled at the weapon, which indicated he wasn't a total imbecile.

"Last chance to talk this out," Terra offered.

"For you, maybe," Marcus spat, then lunged at Terra. She swung the ax at the lion's chest, but before she could connect, he shifted into a gorilla. Now, instead of swinging at a four-legged beast, her ax swiped beneath the gorilla's feet. Its huge, hairy fist with a giant gold ring on the pointer finger plowed into her face.

Terra flew back from the force of the blow. Rather than letting herself crash into the wall behind her, she teleported and reappeared behind the gorilla.

She slashed out with the ax over the gorilla's shoulder. He flinched back in surprise. That was fine with Terra. She flicked the blade aside, grabbed below it with her other hand, and pulled the handle up to his neck.

She pulled the gorilla against herself, feeling his muscles ripple as he struggled. Terra marveled at her own power. She was handling a *gorilla* in hand-to-hand combat. That it was a shapeshifter and not an actual gorilla in no way diminished the accomplishment.

She squeezed the weapon's handle against his neck and felt the hunger of Freya's ax taste the power Marcus controlled. The ax was intended to master *seidr*, to cut through the threads of magic hidden beneath the surface of this realm and all the others. With all the time Terra spent practicing with the weapon, she knew the blade was not the only part of the weapon able to control the flow of *seidr*.

With the handle pushed against Marcus' throat, Terra drained his power away. She wicked away more with each beat of his heart.

It probably would have beaten the shapeshifter had he stuck around for more than three heartbeats.

He changed from a gorilla and slipped through her hands. Terra initially thought he was a bug, but he had become a bird. A bird with a long, straight bill. He landed on the mosaic and hammered away, knocking bits of semi-precious stones and glass free.

"No, that's a masterwork. You can't do that!" Terra blurted as she ran toward the woodpecker.

It flitted away, then before it landed, it was a gorilla once more.

"Oh dear," Leif blurted as Marcus hefted him over his head. He had his throat in one hand and a thigh in the other. He was big enough to wrap his huge fingers around Leif's leg like it was a child's wrist.

Then he chucked Leif at the statue of Freya.

Terra acted without thinking. She teleported between Leif and the statue, grabbed Leif, then teleported again. She misjudged her momentum, and when she reappeared in the chamber, Leif was between the wall and her.

He crashed into one of the walls of the cave. He was barely conscious but still alive.

Terra put him down and turned to Marcus.

"Good to see you care about your friends," Marcus sneered, then removed the box from the grip of Freya's statue.

Terra teleported across the room, reappeared in front of Marcus, and punched him in the face. He went flying, and the box popped from his hands. Terra grabbed for it, almost catching it before Marcus became a hawk and flew at Leif.

Leif weakly batted at the bird's talons, but he was out of strength. Marcus didn't care. He transformed into a gorilla again, his hands already wrapped around Leif's arm. He hurled him across the room, forcing Terra's hands.

She dropped the box and rushed to help her friend. He was unconscious now.

"Damn it," Terra cursed and turned to Marcus. He was a wolf now, with the box in his jaws, sprinting out of the room through the tunnel. Terra moved to follow, but Marcus turned into a bear and struck the cave, causing the structure to crumble.

"If the shape of the cave changes, can you still get out?" Marcus teased.

Terra stopped. She let him take the treasure box and returned to her unconscious friend.

CHAPTER FOUR

Crackjaw's Landing, Mosfellsbær, Western Iceland, Tuesday Afternoon

Harris Barrow's reintroduction to the world of archeology felt like coming home. For years, he had hidden in his home carved into a craggy cliff on the coast of Iceland, protecting his artifacts from the wider world and the woman he had once loved before she had betrayed him.

Now that she was out of the picture, a victim of her own hunger for power, Barrow almost felt like he had been born again. No longer was he stuck in his home, musing over his collection of books and digging around esoteric corners of research. He had swooped in to fill the void of Villon Institute. He had half a dozen active sites around Northern Europe and Eastern Canada, and it felt great.

Of course, the most important was the one on Gotland. It seemed the most promising destination for Freya to leave her artifacts, which was why he had sent Terra there. He was also overseeing a longship discovered mired in the mud and a bog body with rune tattoos, not to mention a few more newsworthy, classic treasure excavations. Barrow didn't know what it was about finding gold or silver, but it attracted attention like no other.

For the first time in a long time, he was all right with that. He found it invigorating to conduct newfangled video interviews over his computer connection and try to convince whoever he was speaking to how important it was to learn about simple iron tools instead of coins.

He didn't personally oversee any of the digs. He didn't have the energy for it, but he liked being connected to all of them here at home. He could rest in his library and let the world come to him at its own pace.

Yet he still found his fingers scrolling through his phone and dialing Mads Jostad.

"Bossman! Nice to hear from you!" the reformed thief greeted upon picking up. "I was expecting to hear from you a week ago. It's been a nice vacation. Malta's pretty when you're not being shot at. What seems to be the problem?"

"Must there be a problem for me to call a friend and check in on him?"

Mads said nothing. Barrow could almost feel him rolling his eyes on the other side of the continent.

"Well, if there's nothing wrong, I suppose I'll get back what I was doing."

"Oh, wait a minute. I'm receiving a call from Terra. Let me make it a threesome call."

"It's not called that, Doc. No one calls it—"

Barrow switched lines. "Terra, to what do I owe the—"

"We were attacked! A giant snake. Then a gorilla! I need to know everything you know about him!"

"About who?" Barrow rose from his chair and hurried to a wall of books.

"About the man who hurt Leif!" Terra exclaimed.

Barrow heard an engine racing in the background.

"Terra, calm down. Where are you? Is Leif all right?"

"I don't *know* if he's all right! He's unconscious. Almost got his brain bashed against the mosaic. Then he *took* it! He took the entire box!"

"Wait, the box? You found it?"

"Found it and lost it! That doesn't matter right now. I don't know what to do about Leif! He wasn't hurt by magic, only pummeled within an inch of his life. I tried giving him *seidr*, but it didn't help."

"Then take him to a hospital!"

"What do you think I'm doing?" Terra yelled so loudly into the phone that Barrow had to pull it away from his ear.

"Well, that's good. Get him to a doctor, don't mention his lineage, and they'll get him fixed up. I've gotten Mr. Jostad into and out of countless emergency rooms. Call me when you know the name of the hospital, and I'll handle everything from my end."

"Okay. Got it." There was a screech of tires, and Barrow thought maybe Terra had found a road instead of driving across the dirt. "Now, shapeshifters," she stated. "What have you got?"

"Wait. Let me make sure I understand. You found Freya's artifact, only to have it stolen?"

"Pretty much, yeah," Terra sounded furious. Barrow was glad he was not sharing a room with her at that moment. "Someone came into the cave. I think he might have known it was there. I don't know. He was a spider, and I tried to smash it, but I didn't know it was him. I broke through a wall and found the room."

"What was it like?" Barrow asked. He couldn't help himself. The Freya statues they had found had all been beyond remarkable.

"It was amazing, Barrow. Spectacular. She was in front of this stunning mosaic of birds, and the detail on her expression? I don't know how anyone could have made such a thing."

"Birds? That might be a clue. She had a cloak, you know. It granted her the ability to become a bird and fly."

"Could this guy already have it, then? Do you think it let her change into multiple shapes?"

"If my memory serves, all that's in the *Prose Edda* about her changing shape is the ability to become a bird. It's the trickster god with the ability to assume multiple forms. This shapeshifter you faced, do you think he could have been a god?"

"I don't know. I don't think so," Terra replied. "We brawled pretty hard. From what I've read, Thor's little brother wasn't known for his street fighting skills. I guess it could have been a fake name, but he called himself Marcus."

"Marcus? I will see what I can find on the name. What else did you notice about him?"

"He liked the color purple. Couldn't wear enough of it. He transformed into a big snake first, and I got the sense that the serpent was his preferred form. Maybe he was compensating for something. I don't know. We didn't get to chat much. He really knew how to throw a punch."

"As a snake?"

"Gorilla. Shapeshifter, remember?"

"Was he wearing anything that could have been a relic like you and Leif possess?"

"Maybe? I don't know. Are tacky shoes an artifact of a god? Or a weird hat? Oh, wait a minute."

"What is it?"

"My exit!" Terra exclaimed. There was a screech and the sound of a car horn, then she was back. "He had a ring. When he was in gorilla form, I could see it on his finger before he punched me in the face with it. I thought he was trying to do some extra damage, but maybe there's something there? I don't know."

"I'll look into it. What about the dig site, Terra? This brawl, did it damage the area?"

"Not too badly. I don't think he wanted witnesses. He used the snake form to scare everyone else off. Got the area cleared before he tried anything. Everything was still standing when I left, though the crew was milling around. I don't want them going into that chamber without me. If news gets out before we have a handle on the situation, it'll be a circus, especially considering Gotland's history."

"Don't worry about it. I know Bengtsson from way back. I can handle all that from here, thanks to the power of the cellular phone. You get Leif to the hospital. We'll talk soon."

"Okay. Thanks, Dr. Barrow." She hung up.

Barrow looked at his phone and saw he had not made the call a three-way but instead had put Mads on hold.

"Mr. Jostad. Pardon me, I believe I pressed the wrong button."

"I know ya did, boss. You ever wonder if any of these artifacts we find have different purposes than we know, except all you old archaeologists can't figure them out any better than you can figure out a smartphone?"

Barrow chuckled. "I wonder about that all the time. We'll have plenty of time to discuss modern interpretations of ancient technology and the pitfalls of assumptions later. Right now, I need to know if you're free."

"Oh, no. A promise of boring conversation and wondering if I'm busy on vacation? I take it the dig's been successful?"

"Indeed. Too successful, perhaps. I'd like you to fly to Gotland as soon as possible."

"I'm toweling off as we speak, boss. I'll be on the next flight out of here. You don't mind springing for first class if it's available, do you?"

Barrow chuckled. "I wouldn't dream of you having to wait to disembark after you land. Gods' speed, Mr. Jostad."

"Yeah, they're who you've got me worried about."

CHAPTER FIVE

Visby Hospital, Gotland Island, Sweden, Wednesday Morning

"It's a bit much, isn't it?" the serpent taunted her. He had spoken in his own voice before, regardless of his shape, but now he spoke in her friend's voice.

"What do you want from me?" Terra asked. Her bracers wouldn't clamp on, no matter how hard she tried. It was like they were made for a different person.

"You are the key to opening up the nine realms. You are the path to traverse each branch of the world tree." Now, the serpent was talking in Beatrice's voice. Beatrice, who had a mansion dropped on her head.

"I don't want to open the other realms. I like the world we're in. I want Midgard to be Midgard."

"And I wish I was a chicken on rollerblades." Then Marcus *was* a chicken on rollerblades. Terra's bracers were rollerblades now, too, but she could not get them to fit any more than she could when they were still bracers.

She tried to skate after him, but she couldn't.

"Bit much, isn't it?"

Terra snapped awake and was back in the hospital room where she had spent the night with Leif, holding his hand. "Excuse me?"

"A bit much that I'm the one in the hospital, but I wake up to you sleeping," Leif smiled. One of his eyes was swollen, but it had already gone down some. More yellow than purple.

"Oh. Sorry about that. I guess I was dreaming."

"More like living through a nightmare by the sound of things. I don't know what a roller blade is, but it sounds fearsome."

"It's not. It's for—never mind. Not important. How are you feeling, Leif? You were out for a while."

"I'm all right. A bump on my head and some scratches on my chest. Nothing much. Not compared to our last battle. You didn't have to take me here."

"I tried giving you *seidr* to heal, but it didn't work. I defaulted to mortal medicine. Sorry."

"No need to apologize. I am not certain you saved my life, but you most certainly tried. For that, I am grateful." He pushed up in bed slightly. He really did look better. The sleep had done him some good.

"Should we get you out of here, then?"

"I would love to, although I must admit, I am perplexed by this…creature. What is it exactly?" He pointed to a plate with a small Jell-O mold on it. It looked sort of like a jellyfish or a sea sponge, but Terra still laughed at the idea that it was alive.

"It's called Jell-O. I think it's made from horse hooves, but it's not alive."

"Horse hooves? Truly? I had thought it was some sort of a shellfish. An oyster from the south or something. So those red bits, they're the flesh of a stallion?"

"Those are strawberries," Terra corrected.

Leif picked up a spoon and approached the Jell-O as if it might strike him at any moment. When it did not form an amorphous arm of acid, he poked it and scooped out a jiggly chunk.

"Oh, goodness! It has more bounce than a well-fed maiden!"

He put the spoon in his mouth and smiled in ecstasy.

"I take it you like it."

"Like? An understatement. It is like nectar given substance! How can such a thing exist on a world in which people try to kill each other? Would they not all sit down and enjoy a bowl of this together?"

"That's been attempted, I think. Maybe not with world leaders. I think most people tended to get distracted."

"I would very much like to see such an event." Leif sucked a blob of Jell-O off his spoon.

"We'll put that on the to-do list. After, you know, getting back Freya's artifact that was stolen from us."

"Curses. Marcus was able to best you then?" Leif asked.

Terra shrugged. "Not exactly. I think the ax would have worked against him. I felt some of his *seidr* trying to take it, but he slipped free and used you against me."

"And you chose to save me instead of protect the box?" Leif asked.

Terra nodded.

"Not the most Viking thing to do, it must be said. Those

who worshipped Odin and Freya frequently chose victory over all else."

"I'm sorry. I shouldn't have—"

"No. Let me finish. I was going to say they did so at their peril. Those who chose their people were the most successful. I am honored you chose me over a shard of *seidr*. I will endeavor to do everything in my power to win it back for you." He leaned forward, bowing to her.

Despite the paper gown he wore, Terra found the gesture solemn and moving, more than she deserved. "I keep thinking I could have done a dozen different things, and it would have played out with us winning the box instead of him. If we weren't in the cave where I had to be cautious, if I'd had Freya's ax when he attacked, if—"

"No doubt all things that occurred to Marcus the thief. It would not do for him to let us win the prize. Better to steal its power for himself before we could use it against him."

"You think that's what he wanted? The power of the object?"

Leif nodded and chewed his lip, thinking. "He was not a god. I am sure of that. If he was, I do not think the battle would have gone as it had."

"What if it was Loki, and he didn't want us to know it was him?"

"Then we would already think it was someone else. Loki does not feint. He feints within feints within feints. This does not reek of his mischief to me. If it is, it is only the furthest ripples of his splash into Midgard."

"Do you have an idea of who he was, then?" Terra asked.

Leif took another bite of Jell-O as he considered the question. Terra heard him pushing it through his teeth then sucking it back out of his cheeks. It was interesting to know not only children did that. It seemed part of anyone's first experience with Jell-O.

"I do not think he was an Asgardian. He did not hold himself like one who has existed for hundreds of years and expects to exist for hundreds more."

"Are you saying mortals act differently than you do?" Terra asked.

Leif quirked an eyebrow and smiled with one corner of his mouth. "Mortals tend to be twitchier than those from Asgard. Not that I blame you."

"You think I'm twitchy?" Terra flexed her pec and bicep in annoyance, and Leif flinched at the motion, still clear under her clothes thanks to a physique provided by training and the magical power of a battle goddess.

"Not you, no. You have the power of *seidr* to smooth out your actions," Leif stated quickly. Terra found it adorable how nervous he seemed to become. "But Mads Jostad? He's the definition of twitchy. He turns to look whenever a door opens. He is constantly scanning for exits, looking for threats. This Marcus was like him in that way. Both seem overly concerned about the perils to their own flesh."

Terra had to admit she was impressed he had pivoted away from insulting her by both throwing Mads under the bus and bringing the conversation back to Marcus. She wouldn't keep bothering him about insulting an entire planet of humans. Not at this moment, anyway.

"Marcus obviously had magic, though," she supplied. "He could shapeshift. Not exactly something most mortals can do. Though I suppose Mads seems able to do it with his appearance easily enough." Terra meant it as a joke, but Leif nodded seriously. However, he sort of ruined the effect when he brought a red cube to his mouth, made a kissing sound, then vacuumed it up.

"Those were not illusions of perception like Mads deals in. They were not weavings of *seidr* like I can accomplish with Bygul's eye. It was a power true and strong. Those shapes shielded him from what we could do. It is familiar, though. Such shielding in another form. I do not wish to say it, but there is a god with such abilities."

"You said it's not Loki."

When Terra spoke the trickster god's name, Leif glanced around the room as if he might be listening in on them in the hospital.

"I do not think it is. However, if there are pieces of Freya's divinity in this world, perhaps there are pieces of his as well."

"Like the wand," Terra commented.

"Precisely. I had hoped the only reason Beatrice had found it was because she had spent years of her time and a vast fortune, but perhaps that is not the case."

"Marcus could be working for the Villon Institute."

"A theory more suited for an intellect like your own, from your world. Though, if there are pieces of the trickster god in Midgard, perhaps he is watching more closely than I thought."

"You think he's on Earth?" Terra looked around the hospital room. She was suddenly aware of how many nurses had walked by. Of the custodian. Of the woman with an emotional support dog she had seen in the cafeteria when she had gone for coffee and a snack.

"I would not dare guess at the movements of a god as powerful as him, but if mortals discovered more than one piece of his, he might be focused on Earth. He revels in chaos. The only plans he likes are his own. I have seen him undermine my great-grandmother simply to prove he could. I think it eminently possible that if Beatrice discovered his wand, he might make it easier for others to discover more artifacts."

"Marcus had a ring," Terra told him, remembering the flash of gold on the finger of a gorilla before it punched her in the face.

"He also had a hat, as well as a belt and shoes combo I could not help but admire."

"Yes, but when he was in animal form, he still wore a ring on his finger."

"When he was a snake, he had a glimmer of gold, too," Leif commented. "When you left, he preferred that form to hurt me with. He also used the ape, but he seemed to have a thing for the snake. I thought a few scales had been damaged and regrown and tried to strike them there. It did not work."

"You know, now that I'm thinking about it, his first form I saw had a bit of gold on it too. The tarantula. It must be the ring."

Leif nodded. "A ring of gold that grants him the ability to change shapes. It is odd because changing shape is an innate power Loki has always possessed. We cannot assume he is stuck in one form simply because another wears his ring."

"Believe me, I wasn't." Terra glanced around the hospital room. A fly buzzed against the window. A big one. Was there a band of gold around its abdomen? She couldn't be sure.

"Whether Loki is involved or only his magic, we must be prepared for the unexpected. Beyond his own jokes, nothing pleases Loki more than taking away from others what they thought belonged to them. Anytime something goes missing in Asgard, whether it's hair or a hammer, Loki is always involved."

"You don't think he's behind this, though?" Terra asked.

Leif snorted. "I cannot say. Even *thinking* he's not behind this means he might be. Though Marcus taking the form of a serpent is odd."

"Because Loki's son is a serpent?"

"There's that, though Jormungandr is so large, it hardly bears comparison. However, Loki was imprisoned beneath a snake before Ragnarök. Skadi collected the dripping venom from the serpent, but when she emptied her bowl, its venom burned Loki and made him violently thrash until he slipped away. Some say it caused earthquakes, but I believe that's an exaggeration. Perhaps Marcus took the form of the serpent to tell us he is not allied with Loki."

"Or to tell us Loki is free," Terra countered, not liking the idea. "Could that mean Ragnarök is coming? Is that why all the gods and goddesses are coming to Earth? Are we…are we looking at the end of the world?

"No, I don't think we need to worry about the end of days coming. In fact—"

Before Leif could finish, Terra sprang into action. Marcus, or perhaps Loki himself, landed on Leif's Jell-O, and Terra would not let him eavesdrop any further. She smashed the fly on the tray of food. Fly guts and Jell-O went everywhere.

Leif sighed and wiped jiggly red bits from his face. "Well, it is a small consolation to know that if this shapeshifter took the form of either the fly or the Jell-O, he has been dispatched now. You are a hero to us all, Terra."

CHAPTER SIX

Good Fun Cabin #3, Brissund, Gotland, Sweden, Late Wednesday Morning

The hospital staff could not ignore Jell-O squirting into the hallway. They showed up moments later and cleaned the mess, then checked Leif's injuries. He was deemed healthy enough to go, then promptly checked out and pushed into Terra's care.

Leif refused to talk anymore until they were in a secure location. "If the fly could have been a spy, surely those gulls overhead may be interested in more than our fried potatoes," he griped when Terra tried to press him more about Loki and his powers.

When they pulled into the driveway of the cabin Barrow rented for them to live in while they stayed in Gotland, they found the door ajar.

Terra's heart pounded the moment she touched the knob, and the door creaked open, not having been shut. She was certain she had locked it before they had left. Despite being informed by the local authorities dozens of times how safe the island was, she could not fully trust the world to leave the door unlocked.

It wasn't so much the people of Gotland she worried about as it was everyone else. Gotland was a tourist destination not only for Sweden but for much of Europe. A vast quantity of treasure had been discovered around two decades ago. That sort of thing did not quickly fade from the public consciousness. Especially when the tourist board of Gotland used it to lure more people to the island.

Terra did not think it so wild to assume a tourist coming here for treasure might decide to try their luck with the precious metals inside unsecured electronics instead of precious metals forged into coins so long ago. She had been adamant about keeping them out. An open door was a bad sign.

It was an unfortunate development. The cabin was the first place Terra had felt safe since everything with Beatrice. They had gone on vacation, but Terra had been watching over her shoulder the entire time. They had been in Gotland for weeks now, and Terra had come to appreciate the rented cabin. Barrow asked if they wanted a larger one, but Terra hoped to avoid attention with a smaller unit.

It had a tiny living room, a cozy kitchen, and a steep stairway to the bedrooms on the second floor. The property included a wildflower meadow in the back that gave way to a pine forest. Though the flowers were not blooming now, she still enjoyed watching the vegetation sway in the wind as she and Leif sat at the little table behind the house and discussed the day's events.

It seemed she wouldn't get to feel that way here again,

though. Someone had broken into her safe space. She'd forever be checking windows now. She opened the door another crack, expecting to see the place ransacked. To her surprise, it was not. Even more surprising, she heard the sound of someone in the kitchen.

"They're still here." She reached into her bag and removed Freya's ax. A surge of power pushed from the handle of the weapon into her body, readying her for battle.

"Will you use the torc to teleport in?" Leif hissed. His fingers had slipped to Bygul's eye. "I fear I don't have enough *seidr* to be useful."

Terra produced a handgun from the bag and gave it to Leif. "Don't need *seidr* to make one of these work."

Leif grinned. "Ah. The brutal, simple power of mortal tools. I do not see why his magical form would protect him from one of these."

"Follow my lead," Terra told him. "I don't want to teleport just in case he's trashed the kitchen. If I can get the handle of this ax against his throat, I can drain some of his power. Then we can get some answers. If he slips away, you take him out, and at least this part of the mystery is done."

Leif nodded. "I'd rather have answers, but if he slips away, I will pop a cap."

"Don't talk like that," Terra admonished.

"I saw it in a movie."

"Just...no. Be quiet and follow my lead."

Leif nodded.

Terra slipped off her boots so they wouldn't make any noise, then she stepped into the cabin. She plodded through the living room, ax in one hand and a ball of fire forming in the palm of the other. She reasoned if Marcus was looking for something in a human dwelling, and they could actually hear him, he was probably in his human form. They wouldn't have heard a bug, and she didn't see how a snake could dig through cabinets or drawers.

She would aim for the face, blast him with a fireball, then get the ax to his neck and drain him of his power. She only hoped things would not get out of hand and the cabin would survive the battle better than the cave had. Although, if she had the option, she would not stay her hand. She'd bring down the entire cabin to get that box and the treasure inside back. Barrow would understand if not insist upon it.

With the ax raised, Terra crept closer to the kitchen. As she keyed to the sounds in the room, she thought the robber was hungry. She heard the *thump* of the fridge opening and the unmistakable sound of a bag of chips opening. Fine with her. If the criminal was calm enough to have a snack, he wouldn't put up much of a fight.

Terra sprinted into the kitchen, ax high, only to find it was not Marcus but Mads.

"You have pickles then, or only lettuce and tomato?" Mads casually asked while Terra yelped, burned her fingers on the fireball, then sent it crashing out the kitchen window and across the back meadow.

"Mads!"

"You really that unhappy to see me?"

"Why did you break into our house?" Terra demanded.

"I didn't break a thing. The lock on the door was easy to

get past. Besides, this is Barrow's house. He's paying for it, and he gave me the address. Plus, I called and texted!"

"You did not." Terra reached for her phone only to find it wasn't in her pocket. "Damn it. Maybe it's in the car?"

"How can we be certain you're Mads?" Leif pointed at the snack-stealing thief.

"You were expecting someone else?" Mads' gaze remained on the ax still raised above Terra's head.

Terra lowered it.

"We were indeed," Leif told him. "Someone who seems better at disguises than you. Less savory as well, if you can believe it."

"Admitting you like someone *less* than me does seem like a stretch, mate. I'll give ya that. As for how to prove I am who I say I am, you want to check my scars? I earned some of them working with the pair of you twits."

"A body would be easy enough to assume," Leif commented. "The twisted mind inside would be more difficult to fake."

"Missed you too, mate. Really. You're making all sorts of questions in my head, but I guess I won't start asking until you figure out I'm me, and Terra puts Freya's ax away."

Terra looked at Leif for an idea of what to ask, but he only shrugged. Then something occurred to her.

"When we were in Greece, what was Leif's favorite food?"

"That's an easy one, luv." Mads winked at Terra. "If I was a phony, no doubt I'd say a kebab, hummus, or maybe baklava. But this idiot has the taste of a seven-year-old and thought the herbed Tsakiris crisps were the best thing to ever touch his tongue."

Leif grinned. Mads was right. Leif had tried a package of the oregano-flavored processed chips in an aluminum foil bag and could not stop eating them. They had even gone out to eat, and he'd requested them at the restaurant.

Terra felt her gut unclench. This was their Mads. He even called her "luv" like he used to, merely to piss her off.

"Sorry about that." Terra retreated to the front door to grab the bag for the ax. She put it away and returned to the kitchen. "We've had a long day."

"I tried Jell-O for the first time," Leif reported.

"I'm sure that bordered on religious ecstasy for you, aye, mate?"

"It was a close thing."

"Well, that's good, but I have to say I'm curious about how you think someone could look this dashing and not be me." Mads went back to putting his sandwich together. Leif reached for the bag of chips he'd taken out.

"A man named Marcus robbed our dig site," Terra stated.

"A man?"

"That's what we're currently assuming, but Leif thinks he might have an artifact of Loki's on him. We're thinking it's a ring."

"Oh, of course, luv. This bloke's only a man, *you think*, except he has a ring from the worst damn god of the whole damn bunch." Mads tried to squirt mustard on his sandwich. In his anger, far too much came out. He wiped it off his bread with a knife that he looked like he'd rather stab something with.

"He changed shape. Into animals, specifically. We don't know if he can take a human form other than his own."

"You saw him turn into these animals?"

"We fought them, yes," Terra replied. "He was particularly formidable as a snake."

Leif only nodded while he crammed more chips in his mouth.

"And he showed up at the dig site?"

"That's right."

"Well, I imagine he can't take other human shapes with ease. If he could, it would've been simple enough to pose as one of your diggers, right? He could have turned into a lion, nommed one of them, stolen their ID, and shown up with their face."

"That is…an excellent point," Leif commented.

"That's because I'm a professional." Mads gave a little bow before putting the bread on top of his sandwich. "Lucky for you, I'm here to help."

"You mean Dr. Barrow paid you handsomely to come here," Leif corrected.

Mads shrugged. The comment did not seem to rankle him. "He pays well, that's true enough. I still chose to be here. A man of my expertise has other options, you know. Other options with less magic, no shape-changing snakes or anything. You two should consider yourself flattered I came all this way. Especially since you're getting paid by the same bloke I am." Mads bit into his sandwich.

"We're glad you're here, Mads," Terra told him.

"Speak for yourself. I would much rather—"

"We're *both* glad you're here," Terra reiterated, cutting

Leif off. "The fact is, we were robbed. And I have no idea where he could have gone."

"Fortunately, you have your old friend Mads Jostad at your service," Mads stated in the English accent he wore so well. "The thing about thieves is that to catch one, you need to be one. People like me, we see what others can't. Our minds are special, and I can only imagine if you'd called me in sooner, I would have spotted this bloke long before he got close enough to strike.

"Not that I'm complaining about actually getting to enjoy a vacation, you understand. I'm saying now that I'm here, you can breathe easy. The only things I'm unsure of are these powers. You saying he can make himself *look* like an animal like Leif does when he wants to dress up like a lady and get some free drinks at the pub—"

"I did that *one time,* and it was your idea!"

"Or are we saying he can actually change into a snake with poison venom, crushing muscles, and the whole nine yards?"

"I think I know how to find him!" Leif sputtered, spraying potato chips everywhere.

Mads deflated. "But I was building to my grand reveal."

"Well, what was it?"

"I wasn't there yet," Mads replied. "Was hoping it would occur to me in a minute, but now it's gone."

"That doesn't matter." Leif headed to the other room and returned with a rolled-up piece of leather. He unrolled it on the table, gesturing for Mads to move his plate.

"No need to be rude when you don't have a solution yet, either." Mads sniffed. "Looks like you're in the early planning stages. I might recommend a whiteboard instead of this scrap, by the way."

Leif poked the map with a finger, and ink flourishes spread across the piece of leather.

"Now, that's a neat trick. You study under Bob Ross?"

"I'll have you know while Robert Ross paints imaginary landscapes, this is *real*." Leif huffed.

Terra had no idea when he had seen the painter on TV, but with the way Leif consumed media while they were on vacation, it was hardly a surprise. Why he'd called him Robert was a question for another day.

The initial splash of watery ink spread across the leather, then another drop of much darker ink appeared in the middle of the page like a brush dipped in ink and dabbed on the back. It spread slowly as if moving along a ripple of water. Its edges slowed and stopped here and there, resolving into darker blobs in the middle of the page.

"That's the view from the airplane," Mads blurted. For all his bluster and talking trash, he was obviously impressed by the magic.

Dark lines crisscrossed the island, forming the major roads, and a few dots and marks appeared. Terra recognized the location of the Spillings hoard, as well as the Mästermyr mire and the chest found there. She thought Leif mostly ignored her when she'd rambled about how important that particular archeological finding was. Yet he'd apparently internalized the importance of finding blacksmith tools enough to incorporate them into his map.

Finally, the general topography of the island appeared, though it was little more than shading where the forests were thicker. Terra knew that mostly from looking at satellite images on the internet. For all their time here on the island, they had been able to cover every bit of it.

"A skill that befits a librarian if I've ever seen one," Mads remarked. "Doesn't help us much with this Marcus character, though, does it?"

"I think it can."

"Why didn't you say something sooner?" Terra asked.

"Believe it or not, Mads' meandering speech about being able to recognize his own kind made me think of it!"

"Meandering? I'll have you know every bit of that was true. There's a code, you understand. A way of behavior that—"

"What do you need to do?" Terra asked, cutting Mads off before he could get going.

"Actually, I think *you* need to do something," Leif told her. "You drained some of his energy, did you not?"

"I guess so, but not much. He was still able to kick our butts and take the box."

"If this works, we won't need more than a smidge of magic," Leif assured. "Every sort of energy has a signature. Freya is the queen of seidr, but all forms of magic are different. If you absorbed some of the energy Marcus was using to change shape, I think you should be able to spill it on the map, so to speak. If you can focus on how it *felt* when you drained him, you can make his location appear on the map."

"Sounds great," Terra returned. "How do I do it?"

"Now this, I'd like to see." Mads bit into his sandwich.

"Well, I would begin by taking out the ax and feeling for his energy inside it. Is that something you can do?"

Terra nodded. She was not certain, but she would try. She removed the ax from the bag again.

"Much of the ax's energy should be *seidr* right now. That is the natural form of magic it creates since it belongs to Freya, and as you are her Chosen, you have been filling it with something similar."

"I can feel that."

"Very good. Now, reach *past* that, or on top of it, I guess. If the energy Marcus wields truly is the trickster god's, it will shift and change, trying to hide. Loki is a deceiver. It is central to his power. His ability to change shape is an expression of that. Remember, he is jotunn. While most of his kind are giants with brute strength who can put Thor to the test, Loki is subtler. His power comes from his knowledge. He knows if it comes to blows, he has already lost."

"So grab the un-grabbable and pin down that which cannot be defined," Mads mused. "Should be easy for her. Do you think King Arthur believed Merlin was as full of it as I think you are right now?"

Leif waved him away, but Terra hardly noticed. She closed her eyes and let her consciousness sink into the ax.

She felt shifting, changing energy, though some of it was Freya's ability to use *seidr* to look into the future. Terra had yet to master that skill. Anytime she tried to peer into what was to come, she only saw options. Possibilities. She could not manifest a future without action. In battle, *seidr* only helped define her motions.

The sense of fate unknown was still in the ax, like always, but something else was there as well.

"I think I feel it, but it's twisting away from me."

"That makes sense!" Leif stated excitedly. "Marcus changed his form to hide, so his magic will do the same."

"Well, how do I make it stop doing that?"

"Focus on giving it what it wants. Let it hide and return to its maker."

Terra tried to let the magic slip into the ax. When she did, it calmed like a fish settling into a hiding place in a pond.

"I can't believe it, but that actually worked."

"Excellent! I didn't spend decades studying tomes for nothing. Now, think of the map as it is, a tool that can help us find Marcus. As for the magic hiding in there, let it know we wish to find him so it can return home. Everything wishes to fulfill its purpose, and the purpose of that magic is to help the bearer of the ring."

Thinking of magic like an animal was odd, but Terra continued with the fish metaphor. If the magic was a fish, the map was a deeper pond than the ax. A place it could hide with greater ease where it might find the rest of its kind.

To her delight, it worked.

A ribbon of red flowed from the ax and into the map, leaving a mote of red ink. At first, it simply flowed around the water on the map. Then it moved onto Gotland itself.

"I think it's working!" Terra exclaimed.

"Well, I'll be," Mads mumbled around his final mouthful of sandwich.

The red mote zipped and moved across the map, seemingly at random. After a moment, it settled into moving along the lines that represented roads. Then, it headed to the western edge of the island, near the town of Visby.

With a thought, the map zoomed closer until it showed the hospital where Leif had stayed, as well as their own cabin. Three blue dots on the map had to represent Mads, Leif and herself.

Which meant the red mote had to be Marcus.

It had stopped directly outside the cabin's front door.

CHAPTER SEVEN

Outside Visby Hospital, Gotland, Sweden, Late Wednesday Morning

Marcus thought capturing the box would earn him the reward he sought, but his employer had been displeased. He'd been less than enthused when Marcus gave him the still-locked box instead of figuring out how to open it. Then, he was downright furious when Marcus explained the reason he had not spent more time in the puzzle room. The girl with the ax attacked him and drained some of his power away.

Considering the circumstances, Marcus thought he'd done quite well. Not only had he followed the archeologist Terra Olsen into her dig site without her noticing, he had discovered the passage to the hidden chamber with the box.

That last part was not technically true. As a spider, he had been completely unaware that he'd positioned himself on a hidden passage, but his employer did not need to know that. Better to think Marcus had figured out where the passage was, only not how to get in, despite possessing the ability to change into any number of beasts.

Okay, so maybe his employer had seen through the little deception. At least that would explain why he was so angry despite them having more of these alleged artifacts of Freya than they had the day before.

Marcus was still marveling at the idea that the Norse gods were real. It had been one thing to discover the ring and its powers and quite another to meet someone who not only knew that it worked but *why* it worked. When he had paid Marcus handsomely, in oodles of silver coins, no less, Marcus had been more than willing to call him whatever name he wanted. It wasn't unusual to choose a pseudonym in this kind of work.

At first, it had been simple enough. Steal a gold chain here, pocket a few coins there. Then his employer discovered the Barrow Company had started a dig here and grown quite irate. Angry enough that Marcus thought it safer to approach the cabin where he had followed Terra Olsen and her accomplice Leif.

It had not been hard to follow them, or so he thought.

He had wounded this Leif seriously, and only one hospital stood within close range of the dig site. He had brought the box to his employer and relayed his heroic battle, only to be insulted and threatened and told to capture the three items the woman had used to fight him. Marcus had not protested, of course. No point when his employer was in one of those moods. Besides, if they were at the hospital, as he assumed, he would find them.

Marcus had grown rather proficient at his ability to take the forms of animals. It was thrilling to have the power of so many forms, all thanks to a ring on his finger. He could have slipped into the hospital as a fly, but what was the point? Marcus' employer wanted discretion, and nothing was less discreet than getting into a brawl among the sick and wounded.

So he had bided his time in his fly form, checking window by window until, finally, he'd seen them. Leif was in a bed, wounded, and Terra had been at his side, distraught with concern. It was heartwarming, really. Even if discretion had not been so important to his employer, Marcus would have been hard-pressed to interrupt the tableau.

However, there was nothing romantic or poignant about them driving home from the hospital.

Marcus took to the air as a fly and zipped above the trees to follow from a distance. All had gone fine until a stupid bird gave chase. One thing that especially interested Marcus about the animal forms was they were all slightly larger and more powerful than their natural counterparts. In particular, the fly and snake forms. The fly was larger than most and had a wicked, poisonous bite that drew blood and caused excruciating pain with caustic saliva.

Unfortunately, this larger-than-average fly looked more delicious than usual to the bird who'd flown up behind him. Marcus dove and doubled back, trying to shake the bird from his tail. He wrongly assumed if he zipped behind the bird, it would get confused and give up. What sort of a fly would try to tail its predator? Apparently, the answer to that question was *all of them.* No matter how he tried to escape, nothing deterred the bird.

Finally, he changed into a bat and whirled to attack.

That did the trick, and he throttled the stupid creature's neck with his bat feet before letting it plummet to the ground, dead.

By then, Marcus had lost sight of the car he had been following. He buzzed back and forth over the road, wondering which of the cabins they had vanished into. He knew methods existed to find such things, like records, receipts, and digital documents, but Marcus had always been a proud analog thief. He stole things from people the old-fashioned way.

His employer was even less adept at navigating the digital space than he was, so he had not been able to offer any advice besides knowledge of the dig site. How he'd found out about it, he had not expressed.

Marcus knew they were down there somewhere, but he wasn't sure where.

He dropped out of the sky and flew above the road, high enough that the wind from passing cars would not force him to madly beat his wings to stay even. He thought he was getting close. The string of cabins below, with paint so fresh it was practically dripping, reeked of short-term rentals. Then, he felt the oddest sensation.

The ring, worn like a pirate's earring in his bat form, started to heat up.

He landed and darted into the woods that bordered the road. He turned this way and that and discovered he could tell where the sensation was coming from. The magic drew the ring toward it, alerting its wearer that someone was looking for it like a spotlight traced back to its source.

Marcus grinned, then used the ring's power to become a serpent.

There was no feeling like it. The way the energy flowed from the ring, through his hand, up his arm, and into his body, taking whatever form he placed in his mind. He had improved since the beginning and learned more all the time, but the serpent form would always be special to him. It was the first one he had assumed, and it always felt natural. Something about being a big, thick, long snake felt empowering.

He knew people would insult him for making such a choice, but not to his face. Not now that he could become a venomous serpent big enough to crush an Olympic wrestler in his coils.

The only person who slightly intimidated him anymore was his employer, who only wanted Marcus to get the ax, bracers, and a necklace from the girl. Easy enough. They didn't even know he was coming.

Good Fun Cabin #3, Brissund, Gotland, Sweden, Late Wednesday Morning

The huge serpent crashed through a window. A moment sooner, and he would have had the drop on them, but when they had seen the red mote on the map, Terra let the surge of power from the ax invigorate her.

When the snake appeared in their kitchen, she kicked the table up, and the huge serpent's fangs stabbed through the wood.

"Ouch!" the snake moaned and was a snake no longer.

"Would you look at that!" Mads shouted, then darted from the kitchen.

"I can't believe he's already running away!" Leif

complained. He'd scrambled toward a drawer and armed himself with a rolling pin. He brought it down, trying to crush the large fly the serpent had become before it could land on him.

"I haven't had time to unpack yet, mate. Give me a minute!" Mads shouted from the other room.

Terra lunged at the fly with her ax. It zipped away at the last moment, and the blade of her weapon splintered the countertop.

Then Marcus was a gorilla. "Miss me?" he teased Leif before leaping through the air, grabbing the light fixture, and swinging into Leif's chest. The Asgardian smashed into the refrigerator.

"This is the second home you've torn apart!" Terra raged. "I'm getting sick of you thieves breaking things."

"Give me the bracers, and I won't break anything else!" Marcus hooted.

"I don't think so." Terra launched a fireball at him. He swatted it away with a huge gorilla hand, and it barely singed the fur. It did crash into one of the wood-paneled walls and lit it on fire.

"Mads on the job!" Mads scuttled in from the living room with a half-assembled gun. He turned on the sink and started splashing water on the flames.

"Give me the bracers, and no one gets hurt," Marcus demanded.

"The only one who should be worried about getting hurt is you." Terra swung her ax, and a blade of energy shot from the weapon and sliced through the gorilla's bicep.

The gorilla screamed and became a fly again, darting toward Terra's face.

"Not so fast!" Leif hit it with an honest-to-gods flyswatter. The fly crashed to the ground and turned into a weasel that scampered up Terra's leg and sunk its teeth in her shin.

She yelped in pain and tried to kick it off, but he held on tightly, then scampered farther and grabbed hold of the edge of a bracer. Weasel claws pressed against the flesh of her forearm while its tiny, needle-like teeth pulled at the bracer. Terra grabbed the weasel and yanked it off her.

It transformed into a hedgehog in her palm, and she dropped it. She spun the ax and shot a blast of energy after the animal. Despite its small size, the magic didn't do any more now than it had earlier. This form was mostly impervious to her energy blasts.

If this meant she needed to get physical, so be it.

She teleported and reappeared in front of the hedgehog. She raised a leg to crush Marcus' tiny form before realizing she was barefoot. The hesitation was enough for Marcus to recognize the peril and slip into the next room.

"Come here, you piece of shifter," Mads shouted as Terra raced into the living room.

Marcus had again taken the form of a gorilla and was throttling Mads. Terra did not understand why, but Mads was trying to throttle the ape back. His arms were at the huge ape's throat, though instead of trying to choke his windpipe, his fingers moved quickly.

Terra suspected the thief was up to something. Poison, maybe? It wouldn't matter if the gorilla crushed his neck, though. Mads' face was turning red, and the veins bulged from lack of oxygen.

Terra did what anyone would if their friend was being

choked to death by a giant shapeshifting gorilla. She teleported beside him and swung at his shoulder with Freya's ax.

The gorilla hooted in pain and tumbled off Mads.

"What do you want with us?" Terra demanded.

"I'll take those for starters," Marcus returned and tackled her.

It was like being hit by a truck. Terra had no doubt if the bracers weren't augmenting her strength, she would have died from blunt force trauma.

Terra's head rang like a bell. Through it, the gorilla's huge, muscular hands tried to peel one of the bracers off like a banana peel. She tightened her grip on the ax and swung it into the gorilla's face. She wanted answers more than anything else, so she turned the weapon to strike with the flat instead of the blade.

The blow was still strong enough to smash the gorilla head-first into a wall.

Terra stood and made sure both her bracers and Brísingamen were still there. After finding her armaments intact, she moved toward the gorilla.

He shook his head as he tried to stand but toppled forward. It looked like he'd forgotten he was still in gorilla form. Though his eyes were not human at the moment, Terra still saw fear and dread there. He knew he couldn't win this. Her strength was greater than his, even in this form, and she had not even drained his magic yet. Marcus was beaten, and he knew it.

Then Leif flew from the kitchen and wrapped around the ape, trying to put a chokehold on his neck.

"If Mads thinks he can choke a monkey, he's not aware of what Leif can do!" Leif proclaimed.

The gorilla backed up and slammed him against a wall.

Leif crumpled to the ground with a halfhearted moan.

Terra would join Mads in calling him an idiot later for intervening when he had, but at the moment, she had a fight to win.

Only now, Marcus understood it was a fight he couldn't win.

He jumped at Terra, fist raised with the ring on one finger. Terra lined up her ax to swing and knock the gorilla out of the park. However, when she swung, he wasn't there. He'd become a fly again.

He didn't even have to dodge. Terra had overcommitted to the motion and couldn't stop. She swung Freya's ax past the fly, and the insect landed on the back of her hand. It was a massive, hideous thing, covered in prickly hairs with a pair of mandibles beneath its huge, red, compound eyes. It sunk its mandibles into the flesh at the base of Terra's thumb.

The pain was excruciating. Worse, the poison in the bite did something to the muscle in her hand, and her thumb spasmed. Only for less than a second before the invigorating energy from the bracers shoved the pain and poison away, but it was too late. She dropped Freya's ax.

Marcus was ready. He fell off her hand then became a human on the floor beneath her. He caught the ax in one hand.

"Oh, *wow!*" he exclaimed, then sliced at Terra. A massive blast of energy shot from the ax and slammed into her chest. She flew into the ceiling, smashing a hole in the only part of the cabin the destructive brawl hadn't touched yet, then she fell to the floor.

Terra blinked, pushing herself up as she looked at Marcus. He was in his human form now, presumably his natural state. He grinned as the ax positively crackled with energy. Rather than overwhelming him, it seemed to be empowering the ring. It was doing something to it, anyway. The ring sparked with the same energy as the ax.

"I tried to ask nicely." Marcus plodded toward Terra.

She noticed his suit jacket was torn at the bicep and shoulder where she'd cut him with the ax. Damage carried over from his different forms. Good to know. Although Terra wasn't sure if she would live long enough to take advantage of this particular piece of knowledge.

"You did no such thing!" Leif shouted and rushed in.

Marcus swung the ax and gutted the Asgardian.

Blood poured onto the floor, and Marcus looked both amazed and horrified at what he'd done.

Then, the real Leif crashed into him from behind, knocking him to the ground.

Leif wrapped an arm around Marcus, and for the first time, he didn't simply transform into a bug to slip away. The thief could not risk losing the ax. Leif got his arm around Marcus' neck and squeezed.

"That's enough of that!"

Marcus roared. It was an inhuman sound, and Terra saw why. His arms, neck, and shoulders bulged with muscle like he was only transforming that part of him into a gorilla. He reached over his shoulder and tossed Leif into the ceiling with less effort than it had taken him to toss Terra.

Then he raised the ax and rushed her, a chimera of ape and human.

At that moment, Mads, who had been out of sight for the entire brawl, shot him in the chest.

Marcus screamed and lurched backward, grabbing the wound in his chest and nearly dropping the ax.

"Get the artifact!" Mads yelled.

Terra obeyed and scrambled toward Marcus, but he stumbled away from her, then crashed through the front door and into the yard.

Terra teleported after him, reappearing in his path. He growled and slammed a bolt of energy at her from the ax. She managed to deflect it with a bracer, but the effort left her arm feeling electrocuted. Obviously, Marcus' experience with a magical artifact gave him an edge Samuel Goodwin had never had with the weapon.

Marcus didn't press his attack. Instead, he shifted into a wolf with the ax in his jaws and ran for the woods.

Terra teleported in front of him while another version of her, an illusion Leif had created, chased after the wolf.

She got in his path. Marcus shifted again, becoming a smaller version of the gorilla he seemed to prefer. He dropped the ax, caught it with a foot, then leaped into a tree.

"Let the bastard go! We can't take him like this!" Mads bellowed as he fired shots at Marcus' retreating figure.

"Stop shooting!" Terra shouted back at him. "I can't go up there if you keep firing!"

"Terra, I agree with Mads. Too many branches up there. If you teleport up, he'll rip the bracers off you, and we cannot risk that."

Terra cursed, but she let the bastard go. Marcus swung through the trees, nearly vanishing into the gloomy forest before turning into a bat and flying off with the magical artifact.

Maybe if she had the ax, she could have taken him out of the sky. Without it, her options were limited to terrestrial ones. Her heart still pounded as she stomped back over to Mads and Leif.

"Why did you shoot into the trees? I could have teleported up there and taken him out!" Terra insisted.

"Maybe you could have, maybe not. It seemed like he had the advantage after he got the ax," Mads stated.

"Is that why you waited so long to join the fray?" Leif demanded.

"Better to wait and land a shot like I did than rush in and get swatted away. Not healthy to get multiple concussions in a row, mate. There's a cumulative effect," Mads stated. "Besides, do you really think Terra could have chased him through the upper branches of a forest like that? She'd land on a branch, break it, then fall and snap her neck! When he got outside with the ax, that was it. We have to move to the next part of the mission."

"Next part of the mission? How can you talk about anything when we lost the ax?" Terra demanded. She was trying to catch her breath and regain her composure, but she felt the lack of the ax's power as a reduction of her strength. She was less powerful than when the fight started, while Marcus was more powerful. She could not see this as anything but a loss.

"You didn't learn anything in that little tussle, correct?" Mads asked, grinning. While Terra usually found his boundless confidence endearing, she could not help but find it frustrating in this moment.

"We learned he can handle that ax," Leif grumbled.

"But we didn't learn *how* he knows about it or *why* he cares," Mads continued, still grinning. "We don't know anything about this guy. Only that he has power that can only be explained by these forces."

"We don't know anything. You've made that clear," Terra spat.

"Caving his face in or filling him full of holes wouldn't change that. We might have recovered the ax and his ring, but who's to say? For all we know, it could be an illusion. He might be some shapeshifting goblin from some other branch of the world tree."

"Do you have a point to all this?" Leif demanded.

Mads grinned and held up his phone. "Believe it or not, there's apps for everything these days. Even for tiny electromagnetic devices unwittingly carried by a shapeshifter."

"You didn't." Terra stepped toward Mads and looked at his phone.

It showed a digital version of the island, with a tiny marker moving away from them.

"I did. When the gorilla was choking me. I appreciate you saving me, by the way. Didn't know if it would work, of course. Then he shifted a few times after I put it on him, and it seemed to do a decent job of following him. After I saw that, I took the shot to scare him."

"Well, that's not so impressive," Leif remarked as they stumbled back into the house. "I could have followed him with my map as well." He unraveled the piece of leather.

While it still showed the island map, the red marker indicating the magic Terra had taken from Marcus was gone.

"Without the ax, I don't think I can reactivate it," Terra commented.

She expected Leif to be glum, but he wasn't. "I am pleased to see modern technology has found a way to keep up with the techniques of old. I think if we decide to follow Marcus, I would also like to use a modern weapon."

"Oh, don't worry about that, mate. I came packing. We'll set you up with something more impressive than a cat's eye on your shiny glasses."

"Let's get going," Terra urged. "If he's smart, he'll get off the island as soon as he can. I'd rather not try to fight a whale if we can avoid it."

They loaded into the car. Mads took the wheel, which left Terra the unfortunate task of calling Harris Barrow and explaining they should have sprung for the rental insurance.

CHAPTER EIGHT

<u>Galgberget Nature Preserve, Gotland, Sweden, Wednesday Afternoon</u>

Marcus walked past the gallows, deeper into the forest at the Galgberget Nature Preserve. He did not want to be here. It was too close to the city, for one. It was also literally somewhere people were executed. It hadn't been used in a few hundred years, but that failed to settle Marcus' nerves.

He wore a magic ring that allowed him to change shape. He held an ax that seemed to heighten that ability and shot blasts of energy from its blade. He had always been superstitious. He'd kept the ring because of it, so believing in ghosts was not a stretch.

It certainly looked like the kind of place that could be haunted. Three stone pillars stood in a circle. Once, beams of wood ran between them from which people would hang by their necks. The hill was situated so the people of Visby down below could see the criminals up here. Marcus could not imagine better conditions for making ghosts.

However, Galgberget had been a park for a long time now. It even had a tiny dirt parking lot and an outhouse for visiting tourists. Maybe Marcus could appreciate it in a different context. The top of the hill offered a commanding view of the shore, the sea, and most of Visby. But nope. He noticed a cemetery down there. He couldn't do it.

Maybe if he wasn't a career criminal, he'd feel differently. Considering most of his income came from stealing from others, he could not help feeling that a few hundred years ago, a person like him would be hanging on the long-rotted beams.

Ghosts aside, it was still an uncomfortable spot for him to wait. It was rather open and a literal tourist destination. It did not seem like the kind of place for a clandestine meeting.

He headed past the three stone pillars toward the forest that grew between them and the graveyard below.

"Between the gallows and the graveyard," Marcus mumbled. He felt like a ghost condemned to this walk. Yet, while the people who'd met their end here had likely stolen *too much*, Marcus had not stolen all he was supposed to. Surely, his employer would understand. He seemed to grasp the nature of the magical implements far better than Marcus did. He must know how difficult they would be to take from those who did not wish to relinquish them.

Marcus would have typically made a point of charging more for such inconveniences. He did not think it a wise tactic to use with his current employer, though. The man had a temper, and since recruiting Marcus, he'd shown more and more of it.

Actually, Marcus almost welcomed meeting in a public

location, even within sight of a gallows. Other tourists should stay his employer's hand. However, Marcus noted that he did not actually see any tourists here.

He knew it was not a power his employer possessed. He could not make people do as he wished. He had never controlled Marcus, only threatened or cajoled. He had not been able to make the Barrow Company empty out their dig for Marcus to investigate, yet other people seemed to react all the same.

Marcus saw no tourists to interrupt them, no maintenance workers here to service the bathrooms. It was almost as if a dark cloud followed his boss, and everyone somehow felt they needed to stay away. It might have been a neat trick had Marcus not been as susceptible as anyone else.

He left the gallows behind as he entered the forest, ax in hand, feeling *more* dread about the meeting despite no longer seeing the three pillars of state-sponsored execution. He told himself it was magic, and he was the heroic lumberjack of the stories and not the little maiden with the red hood. Still, he felt like he was meeting with the big bad wolf.

"You made it," his employer growled, stepping out from the gloom of the trees. Marcus had looked past him but thought he was looking at a boulder rather than a human being.

"Wouldn't dream of missing it, Mr. F," Marcus replied, plastering a smile on his face. It irked him to call this terrifying man Mr. F like he was some temporary teacher from grade school. Nothing about his employer warranted comparing him to a teacher. He was a huge man with shoulders like bowling balls and arms as big as Marcus' legs. He made some attempt to hide his form by wearing a dark cloak with thick fur on the shoulders. It did not obscure his bulk, only that he was a human.

However, Marcus thought he more closely resembled a bear than a human. He'd pulled the hood over his face so his eyes were flecks of light in the dark. His chin was stubbly, with a nasty, jagged scar running from his chin to his lip, where no hair grew. Marcus wondered if he had given himself the scar with his crooked teeth. His canines, in particular, were fearsome things. It would take a team of dentists to bring them back into line.

"You have the objects?" Mr. F growled.

"I was partially successful, yes, sir." Marcus tried to put as much spin as he could on his report. "I took the ax from her before she overpowered me."

The glimmers under the hood's darkness flicked to the ax in Marcus' hand. Mr. F did not smile. He never smiled. He only showed more teeth or less.

Marcus held out the ax. "It has power, like you said. I think it made my shifting abilities stronger."

"Strong enough to take the bracers and the torc?"

"I was only partially successful, Mr. F," he repeated. "I could not get the bracers off her. I tried, but I found no clasps or any locking mechanism. Perhaps you could diagram how they work and—"

"I would not call this a partial success," Mr. F interrupted with a snarl. "I would say you have mostly failed."

"Sir, I would be happy to try again." The idea of facing those three again, especially Terra with her bracers and ability to teleport, sounded like a nightmare, but still better than displeasing Mr. F. "I thought the ax was most important, and with it, we could take the other pieces."

"You should have already taken them." A low rumble emerged from his employer's chest.

Marcus resisted the urge to turn into a bird and fly away.

"I tried to, sir. The ax was empowering, but I was not in control. Perhaps with practice, I might be able to do as you wish. Though I do wonder…" He trailed off, not wanting to tell his employer what to do or even insinuate he was giving orders. Better for Mr. F to demand solutions than for him to think Marcus would dare tell him what to do.

"What? Speak your thoughts. Do not doubt the power of the ax. It is a formidable tool."

"Yes, sir. Of course, sir. I have already felt a sliver of its power and can see its great utility. However, I cannot help but wonder if you might wield it with greater effect than me." He thought back to what he had overheard in the cave. To when Terra had said the word "mortals" as if implying immortals might exist.

Was Mr. F something more than mortal? Was he a demon from another world? A monster fueled by fear, some genie Marcus had released when he had tapped into the power of the ring? It was a terrible risk, but perhaps it would be worth it to have some clue into the true identity. The nature of this man shrouded in darkness who paid him in stacks of silver and gold coins.

"Perhaps it is beyond the abilities of a mortal to handle," Marcus added, bowing his head and waiting to either be reprimanded or eviscerated. If it was the second one, he would turn into a bug and hope to escape.

Yet his employer neither shouted nor attacked. Instead, he chuckled. Or Marcus assumed it was a chuckle. More like the rumbling growl continuously coming from his employer's chest stopped and started a few times.

"Mortals can handle the power fine. You will try again."

"Of course, if that is what you wish. But could you not show me how to better harness this power?" Marcus bowed his head and raised the ax in both hands, proffering it to the cloaked figure.

Mr. F reached out a massive hand. It was hairy on the back, and the fingernails were long, filed to a point, and painted black. Marcus suppressed a shudder. He had only shaken that hand once. He could still feel the points of the fingernails against his wrist. His employer took the ax in his hand, and the hairs stood on end.

"Such power," Mr. F grunted, then swung the ax across his body, inches from Marcus' face. The seemingly unremarkable weapon slammed into the trunk of a tree.

Marcus didn't know much about plants. Maybe the tree was an old one, but he didn't think it should have split in half from a single ax blow. The ax must have sent a shockwave up its trunk. Each half fell to the side and crashed to the forest floor. A hole opened in the canopy, and the vibrant light of early sunset poured into the clearing.

Mr. F released the handle of the weapon, leaving it wedged in the tree's remaining stump. He didn't seem to care about what he had done, as if splitting a tree with one blow was simply a matter of course. He stepped back into the shadows.

"I will not reveal myself to our opponents yet. I would

prefer you continue to strengthen your abilities with this weapon. Then, you might approach what I can do with it."

Marcus hardly heard what he had said. He was too distracted by the fingers of his employer's hand that had grabbed the ax. They were *smoking.*

"Will that be *acceptable?*"

Marcus realized it was not the first time Mr. F had asked that question. He swallowed hard and nodded. "Of course, sir. I can try again. I'll need some time to learn how to use this ax. If you have any suggestions, I'd appreciate it."

"It is not a device I am familiar with. Not like the ring."

"Sure. Of course. I can figure it out, then." Marcus didn't know what to think about his employer being able to explain some magic and not others. Something about that left him deeply unsettled. Maybe because it was more evidence the man before him might not be a man at all. "Let me get the ax, and I'll figure out how to best use it."

Marcus grabbed the ax handle still lodged in the tree and pulled. It wouldn't budge. Not an inch. "Wow, such strength. I can't get this free any more than I could those bracers."

"Not in this pathetic form, anyway," Mr. F remarked.

Marcus would have liked a more supportive employer, but he supposed it was simply the cost of getting paid tax-free in silver and gold. "Exactly what I was thinking," he bluffed.

Merely touching the ax gave him access to a vast well of power inside. The ring was like using a stream. This ax was like having an ocean. He felt its power flow through him and to the ring. He had little doubt that without the ring, he'd fry like a falafel. With it, he could hold on and channel the energy ax into his shape-changing ability.

He needed muscles and great grip strength, so the gorilla formed seemed most appropriate. But the ax had so much power that it was almost daring him to use more. He slowed the transformation, focusing on making his muscles as thick as possible. He felt cords of muscle on his neck, on his shoulders. More strength than he'd had before as a gorilla. He felt the strength of the serpent, the most powerful shape he had discovered.

Thinking about it did something to the transformation, and rather than sprouting thick black hair from his forearms and shoulders, his skin turned to scales.

"Time to see what this ax can do!"

He gripped more tightly and pulled.

Galgberget Nature Preserve, Gotland, Sweden, Early Wednesday Evening

When the tracking beacon on Mads' screen stopped moving, they parked the car half a mile down the road from the target and piled out.

Mads emerged first, with Terra behind him. Leif plodded after her. They walked up the road for a few minutes until the gallows appeared.

A low, circular stone wall framed the area. Three towers of stacked stones rose within it, set about equidistant apart. It was the sort of structure an American apartment might use to contain a hot tub with a pergola above. No ropes hung from it, no sign people had come here to meet their ultimate fate, yet Terra got chills when she saw it.

She had seen it from Visby and researched what it was. It could have been three standing corners of a wooden keep, for all she knew before, but no one had lived there. It was built in the thirteenth century and supposedly used until the nineteenth. They'd chosen this location so the people of Visby could rest assured that justice was done. Or to terrify them into following the rules, Terra supposed.

"They're not here," Terra pointed out. They were all assuming the tracker worked, even when Marcus transformed. He kept his clothes, after all. They hoped that meant he'd taken the tracker with him, too, but Galgberget was empty.

"No worries, luv. It says he's farther ahead. In the woods, most likely," Mads suggested. However, he was not looking at the woods but at the stacked stone pillars. He rubbed his neck, then turned and looked back at the car.

"Mads?" Terra asked.

"You're not finally proving you're no better than we assumed, are you?" Leif questioned.

"As much as I'd like to see how quickly you'd turn tail and run the second old Mads decided to call it quits, I was planning to double back for some heavier munitions. I left a rifle in the car. Should give me the range and power I'd like."

"I thought you had a gun," Terra remarked.

"I do, luv, but there's no way I'll get close enough to use a pistol. Not with the long approach."

"I can teleport us in there," Terra offered.

"I've seen you miss your mark before. No offense. I'd

rather you two go in, and I stay back here, keeping an eye on things through my scope. If you hear a bang, know it was me, all right?"

"Makes sense to me," Leif replied. "I'd prefer Terra to deal with the two of us rather than all three. It should make for cleaner teleportation. Besides, we both know I'm the better combatant when it comes to hand-to-hand."

"If that's what you need to tell yourself before we head in, I'm not going to argue." Mads winked.

Leif's expression soured, but he did not push the point.

"Okay. I'll go in with Leif, and you'll hang back. Leif, give him your map. It will show where we are, right?"

"I got a smartphone. It's all right, really," Mads insisted.

"This is even smarter leather." Leif unrolled the enchanted map and handed it to Mads.

"Mate, I don't care that... Well, actually, that is pretty cool," Mads commented as the hidden pen inked the gallows and the surrounding forest. "Us three are those marks then, yeah?"

Leif nodded.

"All right," Terra remarked. "You'll keep an eye on us and start shooting if we get into trouble. You ready, Leif?"

He shrugged. "You boosted Bygul's eye with a bit of *seidr*, so I'm feeling all right. We'll have to focus on fighting without blasting, though."

"Fine with me." Terra cracked her knuckles. She felt as strong as she ever had, thanks to the bracers.

"Well then, on with it!" Leif grinned.

Terra grabbed him and teleported them to the edge of the woods.

They reappeared a few feet away from the biggest tree she had seen, then moved close together to hide.

"I don't see anyone," Leif announced.

"Let's get closer," Terra suggested.

"Yes, but perhaps I should put up an illusion while you teleport? Being carried along like that makes me nauseous."

Terra nodded. It took more *seidr* to move Leif with her, and she had no idea how much she would need. She was nowhere near fully powered, not after the earlier fight at the cabin. It took time and rest to recharge, and she had had neither.

She teleported deeper into the woods.

"Let me get the ax, then, and I'll figure out how to best use it."

It was Marcus. Terra had reappeared close enough to see him. She leaned out from behind a tree and saw he had his back to her as he grabbed for the ax, which was stuck in a tree. She was tempted to teleport over there, but she needed to know who he was talking to first. This could be a trap.

She poked her head out farther and saw the person Marcus was speaking to. He was massive and wore a black cloak with fur shoulders that hid everything but his sheer size. He twitched his head, and Terra swore he looked directly at her. Yet he didn't come after her or raise an alarm. It must have been a trick of the light.

"Wow, such strength. I can't get this free any more than I could those bracers," Marcus commented. That confirmed this was his boss, anyway, and they really were after Freya's artifacts. It also sounded like Terra had an opening.

The man in the cloak said something to Marcus, but his voice was too low for Terra to pick out the words.

"Exactly what I was thinking," Marcus stated.

He grabbed the ax and began to change.

Terra felt the *seidr* flow from the ax through Marcus' ring and into his body. It changed when it touched the ring, and she could sense it no longer, but she could *see* its effects easily enough. Marcus' shirt and coat faded away, revealing the wounds they had inflicted on him were already the bright pink flesh of fresh scar tissue. His muscles enlarged, then veins coursed through them, and they grew larger again.

Marcus grinned at this welcome buffet of power. He was changing slowly, trying out the power. He found something he liked and shifted. Instead of a gorilla, he became a snake-skinned monster. A demon's skin on a great ape's body.

Terra had seen enough.

"Time to see what this ax can do!" Marcus roared.

That was when Terra teleported to him and threw every ounce of her strength into punching him in the jaw.

He released the still-embedded ax as he crashed to the ground, and Terra grabbed the handle. The familiar surge of *seidr* coursed into her, but she didn't need it yet. She had the power of the bracers. More importantly, he had robbed her of the ax. She *would* have it back.

She squeezed the handle and felt her shoulder bulge as she pulled.

The ax popped free, and Terra turned to face the shambling gorilla-serpent chimera.

Except Marcus' monster form didn't look so good. He

writhed in pain on the ground. His skin rippled from scales to fur and back again. His eyes went from the slits of a serpent to the round orbs of a primate. Both looked pained. His legs could not decide if they wished to be gorilla or snake.

Terra could afford to ignore him for now. She turned to face the man in the cloak—

Only to receive a blow across the face.

She stumbled to the ground, shocked by the ferocity of the strike, then whipped back to look at the figure in the cloak.

She still could not see his eyes. Only a strong, stubbly chin with a jagged scar running to his lip. His eyes were hooded, though Terra might not have noticed them even if she could see them. His teeth drew most of her attention. They were not human but those of a predator.

"You caught me off guard. That won't happen again," Terra told him.

"Noted," the man replied.

Then she attacked.

She threw a jab, another, a third. He blocked all three, which was fine because she swung the ax at his head.

He ducked beneath it, and she threw a knee into his gut. He grunted but did not crumple.

That was new.

Terra planted her feet, then rocketed her leg into his face.

He caught her foot like she was a child, and he was a too-permissive father tired of wrestling.

"This might be fun," he growled. His voice was too low, like a bear was talking. Or a wolf.

"Who are you?" Terra demanded, then slashed at him with her ax. He blocked with an arm. The blade tore through the fabric, though it hardly cut into his skin. It shaved off a tiny puff of black hair and left a red line thinner than most paper cuts.

Despite having ruined his suit and making him bleed, her dark foe did not seem annoyed but interested.

"It's been some time since anyone has tested me. I fear I've grown soft."

Then he lunged toward her with such speed that teleporting to safety was her only hope. She blinked out of existence as the man crashed past her and slammed into a tree. It fell over. Apparently, a full-grown pine was weaker than this man's shoulder.

"You have Brísingamen, then," the man noted as he turned back to her slowly and casually. As if this were a stage performance instead of a robbery and assault. As if he had not knocked a pine tree down like it was a traffic cone in the path of a garbage truck.

"They are mine, by rights. Your man Marcus stole the box from me."

The cloaked man glanced at Marcus, who had finally given up trying to fuse two animal forms into each other and was shifting into a person. He looked sick, like he wanted to puke. Terra would leave him to Leif.

"If the box is yours, tell me how to open it."

Interesting. The man had gone through all this to steal the box but didn't know how to open it? That did not sound like Loki. Perhaps Leif was right, and this really was not the trickster god at work. Who, then? She couldn't believe a mortal had done the damage he did.

"Give me the box, and I'll open it," Terra offered.

The man roared and lunged at her. Terra was ready since she had only been goading him. She sliced across his chest with her ax. He had amazing reflexes and stopped before she could cut him in half. Instead, she shredded his shirt.

Before she could bring the ax out of its backswing, a hand with fingernails like claws was in her face. He backhanded her, and Terra skidded through the leaves and underbrush.

"You are strong for a mortal. You have had practice." The man grabbed the tear in his shirt with his black fingernails and tore the garment away.

Terra had been watching her own body steadily grow more muscled and attractive as she trained with the ax. It appeared this cloaked man had been experiencing the same process for centuries.

He was chiseled, with a coating of coarse black hair on his chest running past his belly button and vanishing into the waistband of his black pants. Without the cloak hiding his face, he was handsome, with a strong nose, icy eyes, and fierce eyebrows. The stubble suited him well, and the scar on his chin only accented his otherwise perfect good looks.

His chest could have been carved from marble and put in a museum, except for the odd scars crisscrossing it. They were not the angry pink of fresh scar tissue. These were old. They were mostly straight lines and ran all over. It almost looked like rope burns.

Around his neck, he wore a stone amulet. Terra could not see the symbol on it, but she was willing to bet it was either a Norse rune or one of the runes they'd found in Freya's caches.

If the formerly cloaked man was perturbed about ruining his clothes, he did not show it.

"What are you?" Terra demanded.

"Getting closer," he growled.

Then Marcus struck her in his serpent form. Terra should have seen it coming, but she had been focused on the cloaked man's physique and what he was going to do with it.

Coils of serpent wrapped around her, binding her legs together and making her fall. Marcus raised his serpent head and tried to bite her, but Terra caught the fangs on her bracers.

She threw the ax into the side of the snake's head with enough force to knock him off.

The snake shook his head back and forth, trying to clear it. Terra must have given him a concussion.

"That's enough." The shirtless man stomped toward Terra.

"I quite agree!" A tree became Leif. Darts of white-hot fire shot from his fingertips into the burly man's chest hair.

He growled and lunged at Leif, forgetting Terra and his own minion.

However, it wasn't Leif but an illusion. The scarred man roared in frustration. Terra used his distraction to crash into his back. She barely had enough force to knock him down, but over he went. They smashed to the ground, and Terra felt his hands on her shoulders, his claws sinking in.

He could wring her neck, if not crack the bones in her arms with his bare hands.

"Let go," she wheezed, then tried to teleport away.

The scarred man held her tight, and Terra did not vanish and reappear behind him as she intended to.

"I don't think I will." The scarred man smiled, revealing massive canines like a dog's. The rest of his teeth were pointed as well.

A bullet hit him in the chest.

It knocked him back, and he released Terra's shoulders. She teleported away, putting twenty feet between them. She thought she'd watch him stumble back and die. Instead, he rubbed where the shot had struck and *pulled out the bullet.* It had not broken the skin. Not all the way, at least. A thin bead of blood dripped from the wound, the only evidence any damage had been done.

"Tricky mortals," the scarred man spat, then stomped toward Terra.

Leif jumped in his path, throwing darts in a rainbow of colors at the burly brute. He swatted them aside as if his arm hair gave him the same strength and protection Terra's bracers did.

She swung Freya's ax and sent a blast of cutting energy at his chest. The bastard *punched* it away. The blast flew through the forest and took off the top half of a tree.

"That might have actually hurt me if I hadn't seen it coming," he mused. "Maybe."

Another shot rang out, and another. The scarred man's shoulder went back, then back again. Neither bullet did any more damage than the first one.

Terra didn't know what she was supposed to do against

this bastard, but she was damn well going to try doing *something*.

She teleported behind him and punched him in the back of the skull.

Teleported beside him and sliced at his ribs.

Teleported in front and—

He caught her by the throat.

Lifted her.

Hurled her.

She smashed into a tree, sending splinters of resinous bark everywhere.

"Enough. I tire of this. Marcus, retrieve the girl."

Terra shook herself awake in time to see Marcus lunge at her again. Compared to the scarred man, he was slow. She dodged to the right, and he sailed past and slammed into the tree she was leaning against. She hit the top of his head with her elbow, and the snake went limp. Marcus wheezed out a breath as he shifted back to his human form.

The scarred man howled in anger, baring his chest to the darkening sky and flexing his muscles in a terrifying display of power.

"He's getting stronger," Leif announced. He was a pile of leaves next to her, hidden in illusion since his darts of energy did less than nothing.

"I guess I should end this now, then," Terra replied.

She teleported above the scarred man and bashed a knee into his skull.

He tried to snatch her from the air, but she teleported away. The clap of his hands striking each other was enough to rustle the leaves in the trees.

Terra reappeared low and swung her ax at his calf. It was a direct hit, and it bit into the flesh of his thigh.

The scarred man did not scream or fall to the ground. He only turned and glared at Terra.

Three more bullets blasted his chest, and he stumbled backward as Terra ripped the ax free with a satisfying spray of blood.

A flurry of leaves encapsulated him as Leif combined illusion and wind to blind their attacker.

"I said enough!" the scarred man roared and went for Leif.

The Asgardian managed to dodge the first few strikes. Was the scarred man slower now? If he was, it didn't matter because he caught Leif's shoulder with a clawed hand and lifted him off the ground. Leif screamed and writhed in the grip.

He threw Leif aside like trash. Leif hit the ground, still conscious but dragging himself away from the scarred man.

Terra wasted no opportunity. When the scarred man grabbed Leif, she teleported behind him and alternately punched a kidney with one hand and slashed the ax with the other while his back was turned.

Every one of the blows should have killed him. Terra put more force behind them than she ever had against anyone else. The physical force should have hacked a chunk out of him, while the draining power of the ax should have wicked away any energy he had. She felt Freya's ax filling with a buzzing, angry energy.

Yet she sensed this power was used to contain. It did not try to escape the ax like most others did. It did not threaten to overwhelm her, either. Then she struck again, and the energy spilled out, hurling her and the scarred man through the woods.

Terra had been expecting the explosion. She felt the power building in the ax. Despite its unusual nature, she knew too much power could overwhelm the weapon. When she was thrown off, she used her bracers to protect herself and managed to roll when she hit the ground.

The scarred man on the other side of the field did not seem as prepared despite the power that behaved so strangely belonging to him.

Terra got up before he did. He lay there, then sucked in a breath and staggered to his feet. He regarded Terra with the same white-hot fury his eyes had shown the entire fight, but only that part of him remained the same. His chest hair, jet-black moments ago, rippled with gray. His huge shoulders and chest shrank. His six-pack shifted, becoming insufficient body fat instead of rippling abdominal muscles.

He howled in frustration and stomped toward Marcus.

Terra thought he might rip the ring off the unconscious man's hand. Instead, he grabbed him by the calf, digging his claws into the flesh, then dragged Marcus off through the woods.

He looked back at Terra only once, and his expression was pure fury.

Then he vanished into the night.

CHAPTER NINE

Bakfickan Seafood Restaurant, Visby, Gotland, Wednesday Night

The hostess told them no tables were available, but when Mads stuck a hundred euros in her hand and raised an eyebrow, she'd miraculously found one in a few short minutes.

It might not have been enough to get them in, as they were, but Leif made an illusion to hide Terra's bruises and dress them all in something more presentable. Her flattering dress showed off her increasingly goddess-like physique, while Leif and Mads wore stylish suits. Somehow, Leif had missed hundreds of years of fashion, only to step right in. His illusory skills were improving. It was about the only piece of good news of the entire evening.

"Do I smell fish soup?" Leif asked.

"Ya," the server told him.

"It smells like home," Leif remarked.

"It is very good. House special. Would you all like that?"

"I'll take the fried fish, mate. Side of chips," Mads stated.

The server looked down their nose at the British accent but wrote down the answer all the same.

"I'd like a salad," Terra requested.

"Salad, bread, and coffee are self-serve." The server nodded toward a counter with the items on display.

"Then I guess I'll have the fish soup." Terra got up and grabbed three loaves of bread and a massive plate of salad.

Mads grinned when Terra sat back down. "I always love it when the Americans upstage the Brits. People think we're rude, then you come through and show us how it's really done."

"Oh, whatever. I got bread for the entire table."

"And it's much appreciated." Leif grabbed a loaf and slathered it with butter before biting in. "It's very good. Not as good as Doritos, of course, but *good*."

"You think that freak with the bulletproof skin likes Doritos more than real food, too?" Mads asked.

Terra looked around but didn't see anyone paying attention. For the first time since discovering Marcus' power, she was not concerned about him eavesdropping on them in the form of an insect. They were all bruised and beaten up, but Marcus suffered the most in that fight. Marcus' boss did not seem the type to eavesdrop. If he was here, they'd likely be dead already.

"I would imagine if he tasted the culinary sensation that is Cool Ranch, he would indeed be as surprised by the flavors as I am."

"Is that your way of saying you don't think he's from Earth?" Terra asked, stuffing salad in her mouth.

"Indeed. I think it's clear now that Marcus has a piece of Loki. The shapeshifting, and especially the form of the snake, is too familiar. But the other man?" Leif shook his head.

"He was unbelievably strong. Stronger than anything I've faced."

"We noticed," Mads intoned.

"Any idea what he is?" Terra asked Leif.

"Not Asgardian. If he was, there wouldn't have been an Asgard. You probably would not have guessed it after only meeting me, but many of the Asgardians can be quite disagreeable."

"Gee, mate, we had no idea you could be real pricks." Mads winked, then gestured for the waitress to bring them wine.

Leif huffed. "Regardless, I think someone of his strength and disposition would have stuck out. I think he could be a giant, though that begs the question of why he wasn't very large."

"Maybe from where you were," Terra returned. "He was bigger than most people. And did you see his teeth?"

"They were not up to the standards of this century, I agree," Leif stated.

"He had *fangs!* Like a vampire!"

"Wait, vampires aren't real, are they?" Mads asked.

"Never heard of the creature, no," Leif replied.

Terra didn't think that was a definitive answer, but she also didn't think he was a vampire. "It wasn't only his canines. All his teeth were pointy." Terra shuddered. "And he had scars all over his body."

"I saw those. That's odd as well because mortal implements can't scar a god. He could be some bastard giant, I suppose?" Leif paled at his own thought.

"What, mate? You make a nerd breakthrough or something?" Mads asked.

"No. Nothing of the sort. I'll have to do a bit of digging, I would think. I'll also look into the amulet. Did you see it?"

"I did but couldn't read it."

"It was a few runes laid on top of each other, so that's hardly a surprise. I have an eye for such things. I'll look into it, see what else I can find. It could be our best clue," Leif mentioned.

"Why do you think he ran when he could have finished it?" Mads questioned.

"You didn't see what happened to him at the end of the fight?" Terra asked.

"I saw a blast of energy that both of you somehow walked away from. Then I saw him spear Marcus like a kabob and stomp off."

"Ah, you did miss a rather key detail, then," Leif suggested.

"He...I don't know. Lost power or something. It looked like his muscles deflated, and he aged at the same time," Terra explained. "But I don't know why. The energy in the ax was different than anything I've felt before. I was surprised it hurt him at all."

"We should not assume it did," Leif cautioned.

"What are you talking about, mate? It sounds like it drained him good."

"Perhaps, but it was a rather long fight, and we all played a part."

"Did you, mate? I saw some sparklers and a breeze, but not much beyond that."

"Fair enough, you rapscallion." Leif chuckled. "I was not at my best in that fight. I'm a big enough man to admit it."

"If that blast didn't weaken him, what did?" Terra wondered.

"The entire brawl. Mads shot him multiple times, you struck him with Freya's ax, and he stopped you from teleporting, did he not?"

Terra shuddered at the memory. It had been awful to be trapped in his grip and unable to access a power she had already come to rely on. "I even tried to teleport with him, and that didn't work either."

"So whatever he is, giant or otherwise, he is obviously magically inclined," Leif pronounced.

"Wait, giants can be magic?"

"Do not forget Loki himself was of the jotunn," Leif pointed out. "Many of them had powers. Some could disguise themselves so convincingly that even Odin and Freya were fooled. They got the giants to build a wall without paying, and Odin got his eight-legged horse out of the deal, but that was not their plan. Giants can wield magic. Any who come to Midgard *must* wield magic merely to exist here."

"Magically inclined," Mads mused. "I guess the two of you should put that on your resumes."

"So what happened to him? He ran out of magic?" Terra asked.

Leif shrugged. "I cannot say for sure, but I believe that would make the most sense. For a being that relies on the forces you call magic, to exist here is not easy. I am hardly proficient at the art, and still, when I first came here, I felt like I was moving through a fog. He obviously had vast power, but to exercise it might have been exhausting. We might have been his first real challenge here."

"That makes sense," Mads agreed. "If that arsehole could survive in this world, he'd be emperor, wouldn't he?"

Terra bit her lip. "So maybe he wants the artifacts to invigorate him? The bracers grant strength, and Freya's ax can siphon it from others."

"Great. So we're dealing with a brute with bad teeth, roguish good looks, and a desire to conquer the world with magic? No big deal."

"Fish and chips," the server announced, arriving with a tray of food. Mads raised his hand and winked at her. She gave soup to Terra and Leif, who both thanked her.

They ate in silence. Terra savored the rich, salty stew, using bread to soak up the delicious broth.

Mads inhaled his fried food and finished first. He wiped his face with a flourish of his napkin and leaned back in his chair, reaching for more wine.

"So we know what's going on. Someone, potentially a giant, is trying to take Freya's artifacts so they can build their power on Midgard. What we don't know is who they are or if they have more specific aspirations than global dominance. That about sums it up?"

"He was angry, whoever he was," Terra added.

"Well yeah, luv. You chopped him with an ax."

"No. Before that. He was angry before we attacked and angry the whole time through. I don't even know if it was directed at us, though. Maybe he has a grudge to settle and sees Freya's artifacts as the only way to do that?"

Mads nodded. "I like the personal angle. What do you

say, Leif? Is there a giant out there with a reason for revenge?"

Leif chuckled and finished chewing a piece of bread. "Only every one of the vile creatures. They see Asgardians as usurpers. They think we stole our land from them, which is a bunch of nonsense. It also must be said that nearly all of them have lost a father or sibling to Thor."

"Thor? God of thunder, Thor?" Mads ran a hand through his hair.

"Is there another less moronic one I am unfamiliar with?" Leif questioned.

"Still only the one," Terra reported.

"He has dispatched several giants, you understand. Not exactly the way to make friends."

"So we're potentially dealing with someone who holds a grudge against *the god of thunder*. Actually, I think I liked the world domination angle more," Mads stated.

"At least we know he's in charge," Terra replied.

"How do you figure that?" Mads asked. She could tell he was playing devil's advocate.

"Marcus was terrified of him. He was willing to risk his life to get those pieces, and yet he hardly wanted to talk back to Scar Face."

"Well, I can understand that," Leif suggested. "That was a power unlike any I have encountered. Granted, I never played sports with Baldr or Thor, but I think he could have tackled them if he wished."

"I think that's a good instinct. We're looking for Scar Face and his minion, not anyone above him," Mads surmised. "I'll start poking around and see if there's been any incursions against the Barrow company. He didn't seem the most subtle gentlemen, but maybe he'll try something besides smashing down the front door while he recovers. I'd bet Marcus has contacts. Maybe we share some. I'll see what I can find out."

Leif nodded in agreement. "I think I need to go through my tomes and see what I can discover. That amulet he had on his neck is significant. I'm sure of it. Maybe I'll find a name amongst the giants. Someone obsessed with Freya, perhaps. Not sure if that will winnow the pool much, but it's worth a look."

"What about you, luv?" Mads inquired.

Terra didn't even mind the pet name. Their relationship had moved past amorous flirting, and now she knew it was only how he talked. "I want to go back to the dig. Scar Face didn't know how to get into the box, which makes me think there must be a clue there. I hardly got to look at the statue or the mosaic before Marcus attacked. If he has the box and can't open it, it might pay to know how it works."

"I admire your dedication to archeology," Mads commented.

"Really?" Terra asked.

Mads laughed. "No. But you history nerds like it when us regular folks say things like that."

"Oh, hush. I'll call you when—" Terra realized she still didn't have her phone. "Actually, I guess I'll go to the dig in the morning after I get my phone from the hospital."

"Busy day," Leif muttered, then asked for a dessert menu.

CHAPTER TEN

Barrow Company Dig Site 106, Gotland Island, Sweden, Thursday Morning

After the destruction Scar Face inflicted on the park around Galgberget, Terra returned to the dig site, expecting it to be a wasteland. She had not checked in on it since they left, assuming no news was good news.

When she returned early Thursday morning after a night in which she slept like a log, she found Bengtsson on site.

"Ah, Terra! It is good to see you. I have not detected any more seismic activity. Thank goodness. I think we might be ready to return to work today. Your thoughts?" Bengtsson

Seismic activity? That threw Terra for a loop. She had expected to come and explain how there had not actually been a snake down in the cave, but of course, Bengtsson had dismissed it. He had dismissed it even when his people were running away from it. He explained it away as a stream of mud and had further rationalized by interpreting the rumbling from Terra and Marcus' subterranean battle as an earthquake.

It made perfect sense, but it still amazed Terra that humans were capable of telling themselves such falsehoods. The truth was too bizarre to be believed. Oh, that wasn't a stream of mud they saw. It was a man in the form of a snake that he could only take because he had a piece of a god. Those pottery shards and coins everyone had been so impressed with? They were nothing compared to the amazing statue hidden in the caves, protecting a magical item for centuries.

"I would like to check out the area first," Terra told him.

"Spoken like an insurance adjuster," Bengtsson returned. Terra did not like his dismissive tone, but at least he hadn't said she was too young or a woman. He'd blamed her old job, which made sense. He might have intended to be respectful. It was difficult for Terra to tell with the Swedish accent.

"I want to make sure nothing collapsed or is at risk of collapsing. If you could please make sure no people or animals come down, I would appreciate it."

"Sure. Of course." Bengtsson, bless his heart, almost left it at that. However, the comment about animals was too much for him to resist. "Animals? You mean like snakes?"

Terra gave him her most condescending smile. "I'm not concerned about snakes so much as burrowing animals. Badgers. Especially badgers. They will investigate caves, looking for good spots to burrow. The earthquake might have lured them here."

"That would be very impressive," Bengtsson replied.

"Especially since there are no badgers on Gotland Island." He emphasized the last word.

"So you think. But how tight are the security protocols? You never know when some creature might come across on a boat."

"I am not so sure—I"

"Look, I don't want to shut this dig down and send you all home without pay. I need to make sure we can continue. Dr. Barrow is worried this will cost us a fortune, especially coming into the winter season. He thinks it might be better to stop now and restart in the spring."

"And what do you think?" Obviously, the idea of ending the work did not sit well with Bengtsson.

"I think I need to get down there and see what it looks like."

Not the most subtle tactic, but it worked. Bengtsson nodded and cleared his throat as he stepped away, making it clear he was not blocking her from entering.

Terra thanked him and entered the cave.

Her flashlight showed no serious changes to the cave. She had photographed many of the fissures and cracks in the caves, and while she saw no obvious changes, old habits made her photograph the suspect spots so she could compare the photographs later.

She grabbed another lamp as she passed the pile of tools. It was the only thing in disarray, but Terra could not say if that was from being shaken or from things tossed and grabbed as the diggers fled.

She moved farther into the cave, down the twisting path until she reached the final chamber and the hidden room beyond.

Terra slowly walked through the passage to the room with Freya's statue. If a room had been damaged, it would be this one. Yet the passage to the chamber looked safe enough.

The statue of Freya still stood in all its glory. Terra breathed a sigh of relief. If this room had collapsed, it would not only make their mission more difficult but would be a huge loss for archeology. Though, if Terra was being honest, she didn't know if they would share any of this with the outside world. They were already drawing too much attention to these artifacts of the gods. Could they dare publish images of this sculpture and expect the world to accept it and not ask the same questions they were?

Maybe they could share after they found all of Freya's artifacts, but right now, it might be best to use the advantage of being the only people who really knew what was going on. The decision made Terra feel guilty, a secret her younger self would have loved to know and would have been angry to learn someone had kept from her.

Those were decisions for a later date. Right now, she needed to understand as much about this site as possible. If Scar Face attacked again, she hoped to have some clue what he expected to find in the box.

She looked at the statue again. If she focused on that, the box's contents seemed clear. The feathered cloak on Freya's shoulder was a thing of beauty. It showed such detail and accentuated the beauty of the statue so well that it could not help but draw the viewer's attention. It could be some sort of misdirection, but Terra knew Freya had a feathered cloak in legend. It would make sense that it was one of her artifacts.

The mosaic behind the statue supported the idea as well. The birds of glass and stone related to the feather cloak. The cloak could transform Freya into a bird. Was there some clue how to open the box hidden in the pattern of soaring birds?

A hawk was the closest to the viewer, large and perfectly detailed in the foreground. Did she need to identify the species? Or see where else the same sort of bird was featured in the background? If she had the box, there might be some clue. Without it, she could only admire the pattern of feathers on the bird's outstretched wings.

In reality, it was remarkable such an object existed. Vikings were not known for mosaics, though the art form predated their reign over Europe by hundreds of years. They were known for stylized carvings of flowing ribbon-like depictions of animals. Like the statue in the center of the room, this work of art was different, out of place. It forced into question not only how prevalent the Vikings had been in ancient Europe but also whether a greater power was at work here.

Terra was one of only a tiny handful of people who knew it existed. The treasure before her could change the entire understanding of the Vikings and their myths. If she shared this with the world, could people accept it? Would they wonder how the Vikings, famous raiders and berserkers, had created such art? They could hardly claim the depiction of Freya was anything but Viking. This was no stolen treasure but something made for the goddess who shed tears of gold.

Terra might be one of the few who felt strongly about that connection since she had met the goddess in person.

Knowing she was exercising a privilege that did not belong to her and breaking nearly every rule of archeology, Terra touched the mural. She had already been slammed into it. Surely, it wouldn't be so bad to touch it, feel what the creators had felt, and make this ancient artifact real.

It felt unremarkable. Bits of glass and stone in plaster. She had felt something similar in an Italian restaurant in Cincinnati. That calmed her, though. To think, these ancient people had endeavored to make this thing to show beauty for years. The proprietor of Luigi's Lasagnas had similar reflexes centuries later and on another continent. People were people and always would be, she supposed. It was a comforting thought.

So it came as a shock when she removed her hand, and the glass pieces where she had been touching had changed color.

Terra looked at the palm of her hand, terrified it was covered in mud, but it was clean. She felt *seidr* pulsing in her palm. What had she done to the mural?

The thought of touching the tableau again came to her with unspeakable desire. The spot she had touched was different colors, but what was it? Terra had to know.

She ran her hand across the blue sky and soaring birds, and they changed. Only slightly at first. The sky still glowed above the landscape, yet it was darker, more bruised, as if on the eve of a great storm. The birds vanished from the sky, and the landscape grew jagged, as if some giant had shaken the topsoil. In the world of the Norse, such an idea was not terribly out of place.

At the center of the mural now stood Freya herself. She still wore some indication of the cloak, snatches of bright, nearly white feathers. A few pale pink pieces of glass portrayed her arm in the same pose, pointing up and ahead. However, Freya was not alone.

Farther back, near a tree that might have been a branch of the world tree, stood a cloaked figure with a wide-brimmed hat. A single glimmer of light under the brim indicated it had to be the one-eyed Allfather, Odin himself. He leaned on a walking stick, a line of black made from imperfections in multiple stone fragments lined up perfectly.

Terra could not imagine the patience it would have taken to find five stones with the exact right line color to form the walking stick. Though the gods were immortal and had time eternal to work out such things, Terra was confident a mortal had toiled at this. Freya might have blessed them with the vision and hidden the work behind a *seidr* veneer, but seeing these stylized representations of the gods felt so human.

She ran her hand across the last areas she had not touched, then stepped back. This hidden mural was not as detailed as the birds before it transformed. Still, it was more evocative, as if the creator knew divinity could never be held in any image, no matter how beautifully wrought, and thus could only be hinted at.

The stone and glass were in the same places they had been before, but a flow of light and shadow materialized and took Terra's breath away. However, that could also be the decidedly more epic subject matter.

In the sky above Freya and Odin was a figure with his

back arched and arms raised above his head. One of them gripped a splash of gray that could only be Mjolnir, the legendary hammer. Flecks of yellow in the glass around him and running to the top of the mural made it look like lightning flowed from or to the figure. A dash of red gave him a thick beard. He was poised above a giant mass that Terra thought was a pile of boulders at first glance but resolved itself into a muscled, warty troll.

Not far away stood another figure, lanky and lean, with the faintest indication of a sneer formed by the placement of the stones that shaped his face. It had to be Loki. Something in his posture looked nefarious. Terra shuddered. She hoped Leif was right and they were facing only Loki's artifacts, not the trickster god himself.

Behind Loki and beneath his feet, as if entombed in a cave, was his son Fenrir, the mighty wolf that would one day kill Odin in Ragnarök. He was bound in bright lines of stones, chains delicate as ribbons, which were fabled to grow tighter the more the wolf struggled. White stones made his teeth into an expression of rage and distrust.

Terra felt like Loki having his back to the wolf was a display of both courage and betrayal. Only a god like Loki would be capable of leaving his own child locked up like that.

Fenrir was not the only child of Loki in the mural, though. Around the mural's border wrapped Jormungandr, the world serpent. At first, Terra thought it was a frame to the image, stylized clouds and oceans flowing around the edge, separating the mosaic from the cave wall.

While the world serpent did serve that purpose in the image, Terra could also recognize hunger and desire in the muscled curls of the water snake. As if this monster wished to use its strength to consume not only the gods but the Earth itself. She was uncomfortable that she had not noticed the snake at first since he blended in with the sea and the sky. It made her worry that if she ever faced this monster, she wouldn't see him until it was too late.

Close inspection revealed the third child of Loki. Hel, goddess of the underworld. Terra had not recognized her as anything but another troll or giant at first, albeit a smaller one farther back in the image. Then she saw the flow of the stones and realized it represented a woman in a dress. The monstrous mess at the top indicated the dead half of Hel's face turned toward the viewer, not the living half.

What she did not see in the mural was Freyr, which she found odd. Freyr was Freya's brother, an important part of the Norse pantheon in his own right. Why was he missing while the children of Loki featured so prominently? Were there more murals down here once upon a time, which had been lost to the centuries? Or did Freyr not approve of Freya having these places in Midgard and want little to do with this altar or the mural?

What did it mean to find Loki's children in a mosaic created with an altar to Freya? Was there some clue there? Did Scar Face have a relation to one of them? Could the amulet around his neck allow him to tap into some fraction of Fenrir's power, like Terra's artifacts of Freya? Terra knew Fenrir and Jormangundr were locked away. All the legends made that clear. Fenrir would not escape until the end of the world, Ragnarök. When he did, he would kill Odin.

Yet Terra had *met* Odin. He had come for Leif and tried to take him to Valhalla when he had faced off against Beatrice over Loki's wand. If he was alive, Fenrir was still wrapped in magical chains made by dwarfs, imbued with the power to contain Fenrir's boundless strength. Did this mural indicate there were pieces of Loki's children loose on Midgard, the same as pieces of Freya?

So much of archeology was looking at tiny clues and extrapolating, and Terra found herself doing exactly that. She could imagine the gods in Asgard above, watching as the people who championed their names spread outward from Scandinavia, across northern Europe, to southern Europe. Then beyond to North Africa and even raiding as far as the Middle East. She could see them watching the Norse spread their name and build shrines and altars to them in more places or forcing local artisans to build things.

The Vikings had not been known for sculpture, yet they had found multiple sculptures of Freya, each hiding a shard of divinity.

Had Loki seen this and grown jealous? Terra could envision the trickster god leaving shards of himself on Earth not to bring glory to his name but to bring ruin to the other gods. Though perhaps even that would be too direct.

Loki would not want to enter a conflict with the other gods and goddesses, each stronger in battle than he would be. Instead of using shards of his own divinity, might it make more sense to use his children? To splinter off pieces of them, almost surely against their will, and use them to bring chaos to Midgard?

Terra wondered what Loki could create from a tooth of Fenrir Wolf or a scale from Jormangundr. Knowing the trickster god, he would not be limited to crafting these objects himself. He would doubtlessly trick the master craftsmen of the Norse and have the dwarfs make these objects on his behalf.

Could Freya have caught wind of these hidden machinations against the other gods? Thor would not have cared about such things, and Odin, with his gift of knowledge, might think he fully understood the situation. For that matter, he might turn his one eye away from it. The legends often depicted Odin as having a blind spot for his adopted son. Could he be aware but unwilling to intervene? Or could his nature as a battle-hungry Aesir have stayed his hand and let such things play out on Earth?

With her ability to peer into the weave of the future, Freya might be the only goddess who fully grasped the hidden threat Loki was creating on Earth.

It made sense to Terra, but it was all speculation. Ideas that might be proven or disproven with new evidence. This was the strength of archeology and the weakness. While one new finding could present new theories, it could also wash away the old.

Terra would have to bring this mural to her team. Leif would surely have insights she could only guess at, and Dr. Barrow would be excited simply by the thing's existence.

She left the chamber through the tunnel and found the last room of the cavern her team had seen. They thought a snake was down here, and they weren't wrong. Would Terra let them back down here? Was she ready to let the world see this sculpture and the mosaic that showed the Norse pantheon like never before?

Hating herself for it, Terra decided the answer was no. The world was not yet ready for this.

She could not face an archeological upset while Scar Face was still out there hunting her. Trying to deny her the only objects that kept her safe in a potential celestial cold war.

She reached into the power of her bracers. The strength invigorated her, and she lifted a boulder and placed it in front of the passageway. She did not completely block it or make it look like it did not exist. She simply placed the stone so no one could crawl through without moving it.

She wanted Bengtsson to find the statue and mosaic one day. She wanted the world to see what was down there. For now, it needed to stay in a corner of the map that had not yet been filled in. It needed to remain secret a while longer so that one day, it could be known to a world that wouldn't be torn apart from the knowledge.

"Anything down there?" Bengtsson asked when Terra reached the surface of the dig site.

"I think it's safe except for one passage that looks like it opened during the earthquake. I don't want anyone going down there until we run a full assessment of the stability. When we're sure it's safe, we can move the boulder that fell into place."

Bengtsson nodded. "I'll make sure the diggers know to avoid the area. The last thing any of them want is to cause another cave-in."

Terra thanked him and headed to her car, still grappling with what she had seen.

She was still unsure where to go when Leif called her.

"Oh, so you managed to get your phone back!" Leif remarked when she answered.

"Don't make fun of me for being concerned when you were in the hospital."

"Concerned? For me? You know I'm made of stronger stuff than most mortals. I would've been fine."

"I was worried you would get sick from eating too much Jell-O."

"A fair point," Leif conceded.

"Please tell me you're calling because you've found something," Terra stated.

"Am I to believe that means you've made no progress on our mystery?"

"I think another god may be involved." Why else would they be featured in the mosaic? Even if it wasn't Loki. Odin and Thor were there, too.

"Yes, well, you've held that opinion for a while now."

"Did you find something to prove I'm wrong?" Terra asked. She didn't want to tell him her theories if Leif had evidence that might turn the entire thing upside down.

"Well, no, not exactly. I did ascertain the purpose of the runes on his amulet, though."

"That's pretty good. Let me guess. Super strength?" Terra asked, remembering how he had knocked down a tree with nothing more than his shoulder.

"In a manner of speaking," Leif replied. "Though that is not its primary purpose."

"Does it make the wearer impossible to identify based on their dental records?" Terra joked.

"Actually, that's closer to the mark."

"You're going to have to explain yourself."

"I believe that amulet to be a nesting medallion," Leif stated as if Terra had the same working knowledge of the contents of the library of Asgard as he did.

"So it's used...to build a place for him to have kids?"

"No, no. Nesting as in it nests inside another. It helps the wearer obscure their magic from others unless they are in close proximity."

"So you're saying Scar Face is trying to hide from somebody."

"I think that is the primary purpose of the medallion, yes. However, they can also siphon magic. I believe it might be working as a lifeline for the wearer while he is in Midgard. Like an air line for moving about underwater."

"Does that give us a clue who he is?"

"I do not believe he is a god," Leif remarked. "I am curious to hear what you discovered that indicates otherwise, but based on what we have seen, I find it unlikely. A god would not need any sort of tether in Midgard."

"Is it possible he was wearing the amulet to keep himself hidden but not for the magical boost?"

"I find it unlikely because of the withering effect we saw. I do not think a god would have suffered so. I am growing more convinced it is a jotunn. They have shown interest in the weapons of Asgard before, so it would not be a surprise."

"But a giant? On Earth?"

"It would explain his strength, and a nesting medallion that grants a different form is not unusual. They are designed to hide the wearer. Sometimes, the simplest way to do that is to change one's physical attributes."

"So a god wouldn't do any of this?" Terra asked.

"Not the ones I know. A jotunn makes more sense. As I said, they grow grumpy and envious from time to time."

"Well, let me tell you about this mosaic, then." Terra launched into a detailed description of the mural and who it depicted. She made sure to explain who was there and what each of the figures was doing.

Leif paused when she finished. She heard him take a breath over the phone as if preparing a thought, but then another occurred to him. "All of Loki's children were there? All three? You're certain?"

"It's kind of hard to miss a massive snake, a huge wolf bound in sparkling chains, and a half-dead lady. Yeah, I'm sure," Terra told him.

"That puts some of the pieces together and could explain why I was familiar with this type of amulet."

"Well?"

Before Terra could get an answer, Leif yelped in surprise, and the line went dead.

CHAPTER ELEVEN

Good Fun Cabin #3, Brissund, Gotland, Sweden, Thursday Afternoon

Terra didn't have time to drive back across the island. Leif was in trouble. At the risk of being pounded to a pancake by a giant with a grudge against them and a desire for things that Leif could not even offer to save his life.

She didn't start the car. Instead, she visualized the front yard of the tiny cabin. She imagined the spot ten feet from the front door, on the little path leading to the road. She imagined the trees across the road, even though she'd be well clear of them. She imagined the little hedge separating the cabin's front yard from the yard next door. She'd avoid that as well. She knew where she needed to go.

So she went.

With a flash of energy, Terra vanished from the driver's seat of her car and reappeared miles away in front of the cabin. She had teleported farther than ever before. She had done it without accidentally combining her feet with the ground or impaling herself with a stray branch. She was getting stronger. Better at using the powers Freya had gifted her.

Whoever hurt her friends was about to find that out the hard way.

She slammed the front door open, ready to tangle, but instead found Mads standing by Leif, who was trying to make a call on his cell phone. Terra realized her pocket was vibrating.

"Ah, Terra, there you are!" Leif looked up from the phone to greet her when she heroically threw the door open to save her imperiled friend. "Sorry. This buffoon startled me, and I accidentally hung up."

"What did we say about breaking in?" Terra demanded of Mads.

Mads motioned to the broken windows and cracked walls. "Seemed like an open invitation to me, mate."

"Well, don't do that! You need to check in with us."

"How was I supposed to do that, luv? Call you on the phone you left at the hospital?"

"I have my phone." Terra gestured with the device, still vibrating from Leif's attempted call.

"Oh, sorry." Leif saw his own face on Terra's screen. "These things are worse than scrying mirrors."

"You two find anything?" Mads asked when they were inside the busted cabin. "I didn't turn up anything on Marcus. I think he's playing it quietly, which makes sense. Means we'll need to keep our eyes open."

"That might be difficult. Leif thinks the amulet Scar Face wears grants him the ability to hide his magic and possibly change shape."

Mads sighed. "You know, there was a time when I

was considered one of the better talents at changing faces. Some new color, a different style, change the posture, and presto, Mads Jostad wasn't Mads anymore. Now, with all you blokes using magic to make illusions and change forms and whatnot, it makes a bloke jealous."

"I'm jealous, too," Terra conceded. "Leif thinks the amulet doesn't grant strength but gives him access to his own power."

"That right? He's not boosted?" Mads asked.

"More than likely, he's at a handicap," Leif explained. "Without the nesting amulet, he would be denied his connection to the magic of the other realms and thus lose power."

"Then we take it off him. We might have a shot at beating him if we let him run out of juice, right?" Mads suggested.

"Not a bad idea," Leif admitted.

"What about his intentions? Why do we think he's after us? It is the artifacts we have, or whatever was in the cave?" Mads questioned.

"I think he's after the prize in the box," Leif replied.

"And what would that be?" Mads asked.

"The cloak," Terra insisted. "It's got to be her feather cloak."

Leif raised an eyebrow at her, impressed.

"How'd you figure that one?" Mads asked.

"A few reasons. The statue in the room has an amazing rendition of the cloak. Also, the original mural showed birds. Some legends say the cloak grants the wearer the ability to transform into one."

"Couldn't it be a room meant to bring glory to Freya?" Mads questioned.

"It could have, except for the second mosaic in the room."

"You missed one the first time, then?" Mads teased.

"Sort of. There was a second image hidden in the mosaic, revealed by *seidr*," Terra explained. "In that one, she wore the cloak as well, though it looked different. Like she was about to use it."

"Mosaic's bits of glass all done up together, right? Sure we can base the contents of that box on what you saw there?"

"You said the children of Loki were in that image as well, correct?" Leif asked.

"That's right," Terra replied.

"I think that is another indication the cloak was there. Of all Freya's artifacts, the cloak might be the most famous on Midgard, correct?"

"I would say so, yes," Terra agreed. "Though I'm an archeology nerd and always thought her golden tears were the most interesting."

"What do Loki's children have to do with it?" Mads asked.

"Several gods have used Freya's cloak. It's beautiful and grants transformation abilities. Even Loki used it despite having the ability to transform himself. I believe depicting him alone might not have indicated as much, but showing the trickster god and his children makes that part of the lore around Freya salient."

"So it's Loki, then," Mads suggested. "Right? It's got to

be. He stole the cloak before, and now he wants it again. Even had his mugshot down there."

"I'm with Mads. That's the most obvious answer to who has been following us."

"Loki doesn't fight the way that man did," Leif pointed out.

"What if he didn't want us to think it was him? The old double-play. If that was the case, nothing would make more sense than him punching you around like he did," Mads posited.

"It is a possibility. I will not rule it out, but I doubt it," Leif replied. "Loki is a trickster, a being of chaos and mischief. I don't see why he'd go through these intermediaries. If he chose to fight, I don't know why he would have withered away. I think it is a jotunn. A jotunn with a relation to Loki perhaps, or at least an understanding of the history." His eyes widened, and he paled. "I think I know who it is."

"Who, mate?" Mads demanded.

"It is a jotunn, as I said, with a connection to Loki. Though I should have considered that option sooner. Of course, there will be hell to pay in Asgard if I'm right."

"Right about what?" Terra insisted.

Then, she nearly teleported away in surprise when a knock came at the door.

Mads said nothing. He went to the spot beside the door and drew a handgun.

Leif turned his head like a dog hearing something outside. Before Terra could say anything, he answered the door.

"Hello! My name is Byerg Stergen, and the cabin's

owner sent me to assess the damages and start the repair process."

Terra got a bad feeling in her gut, and Mads kept his hand on his gun.

Leif—trusting, otherworldly Leif—clapped the man on the shoulder and led him inside.

CHAPTER TWELVE

Good Fun Cabin #3, Brissund, Gotland, Sweden, Thursday Afternoon

"Surge Byergen, was it?" Leif kept his arm around the repairman's shoulder as he led him inside the house.

"Byerg Stergen," Byerg corrected. "It's a common mistake. I won't be long. Only need to take some measurements. These windows won't replace themselves!"

His accent was odd. It was hard for Terra to parse out Northern European accents, but Byerg's did not sound Swedish. She looked at Leif, trying to convey that she did not trust this person, but Leif was oblivious to her signals.

"I'm so impressed that you're here already. We hardly had time to tell our employer what happened."

"Ah, yes. The Barrow Company got in touch with the owner, and they got in touch with me. You know we must have all this fixed before winter sets in, or there's nothing to be done about it if the water gets in." Byerg shook his head in dismay.

Mads gestured from behind Byerg's back that they

should definitely murder the man. He kept mouthing "Barrow Company" and making cutting motions across his neck. They had not used the Barrow Company to rent this cabin but a shell corporation because they had been paranoid about being tracked here.

They had explained all this to Leif, but he must not have been paying attention when they got into the weeds of using receipts and internet transactions to track their whereabouts.

Terra didn't know what to do. Leif still had an arm around Byerg like they were old friends. Mads couldn't shoot, and Terra didn't want to teleport over and risk making Leif flinch.

But before Terra could act, Leif did.

With his arm still around Byerg's shoulder, he brought his other hand to his face, created a ball of light, and threw it into his eyes.

Byerg screamed and stumbled backward over Leif's leg, which he had extended to trip him. The man crashed to the ground, and with a quick jab to his face, he was unconscious.

"What in the fuck was that, mate?" Mads demanded, sounding more impressed than angry.

"Was it not obvious he was Marcus, the malcontent, in disguise?" Leif asked.

"I thought Marcus could only turn into animals," Terra remarked.

"Perhaps his time with the ax helped improve his abilities," Leif suggested. "However, unless our repairman makes a habit of working with bears to fix homes, I think this is our man."

He pulled up the repairman's pant leg to reveal claw marks. They were bright pink, freshly healed, but they had all seen Marcus' shapeshifting power grant him healing abilities.

"I'd be willing to wager a bag of candy that he also has a slash on his bicep and shoulder and a gunshot wound somewhere up there, where Mads struck him."

"Good show, mate, good show!" Mads enthused. "But do you have X-ray vision or something? How did you know about his leg?"

"A lucky guess. I deduced he was an imposter, though."

"I thought you believed every word he said," Terra challenged.

"Well, that was my intention, of course. When I saw the two of you react, I knew you had not called for food delivery, let alone a repairman. Furthermore, if Harris had hired the man, he would have sent word through the cellular phones. He knows we are on high alert and would not wish to surprise us."

"He could have been a regular repairman, though," Terra pointed out. "The house looks pretty bad. He could have been looking for work."

"Is that so?" Leif looked abashed for the first time. "With your phones and internet, I had assumed the times of door-to-door sales were over. People coming to your door can be awkward, even in Asgard. I had assumed you were past all this. That blast I hit him with should not have caused any permanent damage, though. He would have come to and remembered nothing."

"Very impressed, mate. I'm beginning to feel like you're getting the hang of things around here!"

"Well, thank you, Mr. Jostad. You have been an excellent, if unorthodox, teacher."

"What now?" Terra asked.

"Now we need to strip him," Leif announced with a gleam in his eyes.

"Ah, still a bit of that old-school debauchery to work through," Mads added.

"No, not for anything like that. However, I can attest that shapeshifters tend to make fine lovers. They want to impress, so they are giving and can take any shape you imagine. That being the fun of it, it's hardly worth holding back."

"Coming back to the man you punched in the face. Why do you want to strip him?" Terra asked.

Leif lifted his hand. "No ring. Either it's not the object we thought it was, or he's keeping it somewhere else."

"By all means, mate. Who am I to stand between a Viking and his plunder?"

Terra pulled Marcus' shirt off. He did have scars that matched where Terra had struck his gorilla form with her ax. Both wounds already looked healed, like they had happened a year ago instead of this week.

"I think I found something," Terra stated, but not quickly enough to prevent Leif from yanking off Marcus' pants.

"You can't hide anything from us!" Leif crowed into the confines of the tiny cabin.

"Are you hoping he would have zebra legs or a horse—l"

"You guys, look," Terra insisted.

Mads and Leif looked. Terra could not decide which of their faces was more aghast.

"Oh, for the love of…that's not right." Mads moaned.

"I suppose that's one way to solve the problem of where to hide the ring," Leif managed.

A finger sprouted from Marcus' abdomen, lying along one of his ribs. It had three bones and three joints, counting where it affixed to Marcus' torso. It even had a fingernail, and those little wrinkles all fingers have when people extend them. It was a normal finger, only growing from his hand. Something about its placement was deeply unsettling and made Terra wonder what types of things Leif had been asking shapeshifters to do.

"Mads, pluck it off," Terra ordered.

"Me? Why me? I don't want to touch that thing!"

"You're a pickpocket," Terra pointed out. "If he tries anything, Leif already proved he knows how to punch him hard enough to knock him out, and I'll slice him with my ax." She teleported to where she had left the weapon, picked it up, and reappeared in less than a second.

"You are getting good at that," Leif agreed.

"Good enough not to waste my skills fondling weird fingers. Mads?"

"Fine. Though I don't appreciate you saying that word before I touch it. It's not what I'm about, mate. Fondling. Sounds like something this librarian would do to a first edition, not something befitting—"

"Mads!"

"Right, right." In a blink and a flourish of Mads' hand, the ring was no longer on Marcus' extra finger. As soon as it broke contact with his skin, the finger shrank back into his body, leaving not even a blemish to mark its temporary existence. Shapeshifters were weird.

Mads seemed to agree because he immediately gave the ring to Leif. "I'll stick with the mortal stuff from the twenty-first century, thank you very much."

"Quite." Leif held the ring in his palm and eyed it warily.

"Why didn't he do that before?" Mads asked after he'd fetched a chair and duct tape.

Terra lifted the still-unconscious Marcus into position, and Mads duct-taped his ankles and wrists to the chair and his arms to his sides.

"I don't think he was able to," Terra suggested. "When he was a gorilla, he wore it on his finger. He had a gold band around him when he was a snake, although I thought it was a stripe. Even the tarantula form I first saw had a gold band."

"So why grow this little protuberance?" Mads asked.

"Because he can, thanks to the power of Freya's ax," Terra explained.

"You think he had it long enough to rub off on him?" Leif asked.

"How else do you explain that thing?" Terra pointed at where the other finger had been. "Since I came into contact with the artifacts, I've been able to access some of those abilities without directly touching them, especially the strength from the bracers."

"Hmm. Maybe because you've had them the longest?" Leif asked.

"That's what I'm thinking, yeah," Terra confirmed.

"But he didn't have the ax that long," Mads pointed out.

"Right, but the ax is the most powerful and the most diverse as far as the magic it can control. Brísingamen grants the wearer teleportation, and the bracers grant strength and some other secondary powers, mostly energy and illusions. The ax can undo any of that, as well as create blasts of its own. When I hold it, I feel stronger, faster. I can tap into *seidr* more efficiently. He must have used it to augment the ring's powers. That was how he formed into that half-gorilla, half-snake monster."

"And how he grew that little nubbin." Mads shivered.

"A less impressive, though more useful application of the power, I would say," Leif chimed in.

"I thought that sort of thing would impress you for certain, mate," Mads suggested.

"Mads, can you check and see if there's any bleach under the sink?"

"Bleach? First, I learn Leif has the leanings of the Dark Age torturers. Now I discover you know some of the best chemical torture techniques? It's a new day for you two!"

"I don't want to torture anyone! I only want answers."

"That's what they all say before the torture. Classic part of the old Mutt and Jeff technique. You dip his hand in the bleach, it starts to burn. You say this could go on all day. Then I come in and admonish you, get him some water, tell him how much it hurts me to see this, and a couple of answers could end it."

"We're not doing anything like that!"

"I understand you'd want to be the nice bloke, and normally, I would agree, what with you having the pretty face and all. The thing is, he already knows you're the tough of the bunch."

Terra huffed. "I only want the smell to wake him up."

"Oh!" Mads grinned. "Why didn't you say so?"

"If you wish to wake him with the wonders of aroma, allow me." Leif rubbed Bygul's eye. It sparkled when he touched it, and Terra held her nose, preparing for the Norse equivalent of bleach.

Instead, the aroma of citrus and cinnamon filled the room, growing in strength and intensity until Marcus snorted, lifted his head, and blinked awake.

"Wazzat?" he mumbled thickly. "Someone making scones?"

"We are, mate. If you're willing to cooperate with us, we'll give you the most delicious fresh-baked scone you want. Right, Terra?" Mads winked at her.

Terra was in no mood to pantomime a good-cop, bad-cop routine, but she supposed she had no choice now. She wouldn't be nice to Marcus. Not after he had robbed them, fought them, and tried to sneak into their cabin.

"Tell us who you're working for, and we'll untie you," Terra spat.

Marcus went rigid at the sound of Terra's voice, then met her eyes. Even bound as he was, he remained defiant.

"You think duct tape can contain me? You think these modern contrivances can stand against the ancient power of the serpent?" Marcus flexed. The duct tape moved only slightly, and he looked around in confusion.

"You done, mate? A scone could be yours, but not if you're going to keep messing around."

"Perhaps I don't have the power to become a serpent and break these bonds, and instead will become a biting fly you will never be able to capture!" Marcus actually made a buzzing sound, but it did not help him transform.

"You are looking for this, I assume?" Leif held up the ring between thumb and forefinger.

"Oh…oh, shit." Marcus wilted. He looked down and seemed to fully understand his situation for the first time. He was mostly naked, bound to a chair, and surrounded by people he had turned into his enemies. "You wouldn't happen to have one of those scones?"

CHAPTER THIRTEEN

Good Fun Cabin #3, Brissund, Gotland, Sweden, Thursday Afternoon

"The scones were a lie, mate. Even if they weren't, we wouldn't give them to someone who tried to turn into a snake and murder us."

"I wasn't going to murder you," Marcus whimpered.

"Only rob us, then?" Terra pressed.

Marcus couldn't even shrug properly. "Only because I didn't have a choice. You would have done the same thing in my position!"

"What position is that?" Leif asked.

"Oh, not this again," Mads muttered.

"I didn't have a choice! I thought the ring was a gift, but it turned into a curse."

"You mean when your boss found you," Terra stated.

Marcus nodded. "You'll see. He won't stop. He never stops, and he's stronger than you can imagine. *More* than you can imagine."

"Who is he?" Terra demanded. "And don't try to lie to us. Mads will see right through you."

"Why lie? You'll find out soon enough. I didn't think others would believe it, but considering you can teleport and face me when I transform, maybe you won't doubt it," Marcus muttered toward the floor. He was speaking too quickly, vomiting out the words in a confession.

"Give us the name," Mads insisted. "Maybe I'll find a little something for you to nosh."

Marcus raised his head and looked Terra in the eye. "The man you fought near the gallows was none other than the god Loki's son, Fenrir Wolf."

"I knew it!" Leif proclaimed.

"Oh, come off it, mate. You knew no such thing," Mads retorted.

"I said it was a jotunn! Fenrir, son of Loki, has the blood of a giant in him."

"I don't know. I'm with Mads on this. Saying it was a giant is like saying Beatrice was a human."

"But I said he likely had a connection to Loki!"

"That's not the same as saying it's his son, who I thought was an actual wolf, by the way," Mads remarked.

"Oh, he's a wolf, all right," Marcus murmured.

"If you thought it was Fenrir this whole time, why didn't you say anything?" Terra asked.

"Because technically, it should not be possible. Fenrir is supposed to be imprisoned after his defeat at Ragnarök. You cannot kill the Allfather and expect to walk around freely. Even the gods take that sort of thing seriously," Leif proclaimed.

Terra's mind was spinning. They were facing Fenrir.

Fenrir Wolf, who was supposed to be bound in magic cords until the end of days when the final battle happened, and he escaped and killed Odin. Only the end of days had somehow *already happened?*

"Well, he's definitely not imprisoned." Marcus tried to shrug, though the duct tape stifled the movement. "Mad, though."

"I would expect so," Leif responded. "Vidarr *killed* him and was made a hero over the whole ordeal. Not very pleasant for Fenrir."

"I thought you said Vidarr killed Fenrir." Mads frowned.

"That would explain why he mutters that name sometimes," Marcus put in. "It's part of his litany. He doesn't like Thor or Odin much, either. Though I don't think he really likes anything."

"How can he be here if he's *dead?*" Mads demanded. "And for that matter, didn't the two of you meet Odin after we danced with Beatrice?"

"Wow. You three run in some interesting circles," Marcus mused. Leave it to a professional thief to be more interested in the name of an antiquities dealer than literal Norse gods. It made sense, though. Marcus had probably tried to steal from the Villon Institute, while this was likely his first time intentionally stealing something that belonged to a goddess. Yet he was taking their existence with less surprise than Terra felt at Leif's admission that Ragnarök was…what, old news?

"Leif, wait. Can you please go back to the part about Ragnarök? Are we talking end-of-the-world Ragnarök?

"Is there another I am unaware of?" Leif asked.

"Well, considering it was supposed to be *the end,* I'm confused on the timeline here. When *exactly* did the final battle come to pass?"

Leif shrugged. "Some time ago. A century, maybe three? To be perfectly frank, I think we might have overhyped that a tad."

"You over*hyped* the end of the world?" Mads asked, as dumbfounded as Terra.

"I like you lot," Marcus piped up. "I've been in tight spots before, but this is the first time anyone has tried to torture me with mythology."

"Quiet, or we'll try bleach," Mads barked.

Marcus swallowed and nodded.

"How is the world already over?" Terra asked.

"Is this, like, all a dream? Odin's dream? Oh, no, wait. You said he's dead. Freya's dream, then? Oh dear god, is this *your* dream?" Mads looked at Leif, fear in his eyes.

"I assure you my dreams do not consist of rehashing old news. It was all an error of translation, which I may have played some small part in supporting."

"You...what?"

"It was an honest mistake. One I'm sure Freya herself might have made in my position if the gods could be bothered to translate the cryptic prophecies of the Norns, that is."

Wind rattled the tiny cabin, blowing leaves through the broken window.

Leif cleared his throat and looked put out. "My great-grandmother would have had more important things to do than translate poetry. Like she surely must have more important things to do right now than listen to this."

No wind came that time, and Leif looked mollified.

"You were saying how you messed up Ragnarök," Mads prompted.

"I did no such thing. The battle did come to pass, and much of what the Norns said was to happen did indeed happen. It was simply not the end of the world. It's really Skuld's fault. Of the three of them, she was always the hardest to understand.

"Urd talked like a grandmother from the last generation despite being as comely as the other two, and Verdandi always spoke normally. Skuld used words that hadn't been invented yet. I did my best to translate the words. But what is an eon, *really*? Or an age? Is the end of an age so different from the end of the world?"

"Apparently so," Mads murmured.

Leif wilted. "Well, hindsight being clearer than foresight, I agree. They might have fact-checked me. I was millennia younger than them, but they're all gods of battle. The idea of a final war appealed to all of them, especially Thor, being the brute he is. But Freya, too. The only ones not on board for the battle were Loki and the other Jotunn. We all thought that was a trick, though."

"You said Odin *died*," Terra insisted.

"I did, yes. Err, *he* did, rather. Killed by Fenrir. His neck was bitten through, or so said the poets who witnessed the ordeal. I rather suspect it was only *most of the way* through. Poets are prone to exaggerations, of course."

"But we *met* him! His neck was intact!"

"Quite. Because he is Odin. He who hung from the branch of Yggdrasil for nine days and nine nights until the branch broke, and he rose after death. He who took out his own eye in exchange for knowledge. He who threw himself on his spear, Gungnir, to prove a point. Or win a bet, I suppose, depending on the teller of that particular tale. He has died before, and he will die again."

"You say that like it's nothing," Mads remarked.

Leif shrugged. "Not *nothing*. The end of an age or an era, but not the end of the world. He lay dead for nine more days after the battle with Fenrir, but he rose again in the dawn. Fenrir took much longer to come back!"

"Fenrir, who I fought." Terra could hardly believe it.

"He's not the sort of gentleman people name their children after, is he?" Leif retorted. "I assume he is the very same, yes."

"But the zombie version?" Mads asked.

"Hardly. I had no idea you liked these Romero films, Mads. We should watch a few when this is all over."

"You're saying even though he came back from the dead, he's not a zombie," Terra persisted.

"Of course not. Many of the gods died in that battle. Thor was poisoned by Jormangundr and fell dead nine steps after defeating the world serpent, while Heimdall slayed Loki himself. I didn't get any of that wrong. Names are names, and they're easy enough to understand.

"The waves crashed upon the shores, and Surtr's great flaming sword set fire to every forest on Earth. Or so said Heimdall before he went off to stab Loki, and we tended to trust him, what with all the smoke. We all really believed it was the end, you understand, until Odin got back up."

"After nine days?" Terra blurted.

Leif shrugged again. "Nine days in Asgard is a different thing than nine days on Midgard. We live by the pulse of

Yggdrasil that supports all things. You humans count the spins of the Earth. Days are similar, but different."

"But how can he get back up when his neck is chopped through?" Mads pressed.

"What is a neck to a god? Or a pulse? Or a body? Odin can change form, and Thor has the power of thunder in his veins. Perhaps something could end them, but the stopping of their heart? Hardly."

"So Odin gets back up after nine days or nine hundred years, and everyone realizes the world is going to keep on going?"

"Indeed. Until it happens again. However, by this time, it hardly made sense to keep everyone in the places they escaped from. Hel was allowed to continue to rule the dead. Who else would want to do it? But Fenrir? We can hardly capture him and bind him in the chains the dwarves made. How would that even work? Can you imagine Tyr offering to put his *other* hand in Fenrir's mouth?" Leif was the only one of them to chuckle at the image.

"And Fenrir?" Terra asked.

"We knew he could not be bound. The only one who could trick him into that would be his father, who refused to immobilize his son. He offered a solution, though. If Fenrir would leave Asgard via the world tree, he was promised to be master of a realm of great power. No one would bind him as long as he resided there. He took the deal, and Thor led him to Niflheim."

"Niflheim?" Mads asked.

"A realm of icy mist and cold darkness. Isn't the land of the dead supposed to be there?" Terra asked.

"Indeed! You really do know your mythology. When

Fenrir discovered the realm of great power was in fact the realm of his sister, Hel, he became enraged. Unsurprising, really. He refused to defeat her and claim her realm for his own and demanded Thor take him home back the way they had come."

"Going to take a wild guess here and assume Thor refused," Mads suggested.

"Precisely. He likely would have said yes. Thor is not the type to invent deceptions on his own. However, he had been told not to. Instead, he destroyed the branch of the World Tree they had used to get there and flew off in his chariot, and Heimdall sent the Bifrost for him. Fenrir has been trying to escape ever since, but any time he comes close to a branch or a root, whoever is on guard duty destroys it. Whoever allowed him out must be in a great deal of trouble."

"You're saying the great warrior gods of legend have to babysit Loki's pup in shifts?" Mads asked.

"You do have a way with words, Mr. Jostad, do you not? I never would have phrased it in such a way, yet that is the gist of it."

"Wait. All this stuff, my ring, your ax—all of it really belongs to the gods?" Marcus looked both stupefied and terrified.

"You didn't think something might be amiss when it turned out you could *transform?*" Mads questioned.

Marcus grinned. "I didn't realize any of that for a while."

"How did you find Loki's ring?" Terra asked.

"It really is his?" Marcus countered.

"We have no reason to think otherwise. It is an object of

great power associated with a deity with the same ability. To assume it is anyone other than the trickster god's would be folly," Leif explained.

Marcus nodded and swallowed. "It's just he sounds like he might be worse than Fenrir. Especially if he helped trick his own son into being stuck in…whatever you said. Nipplehelm."

Leif snorted. "Niflheim."

"The ring. Did you steal it from a dig site as well?" Terra demanded more forcefully.

"No, ma'am. Not at all. Part of a regular heist. A German millionaire. Helped improve the fuel pump or something, I don't know," Marcus babbled. This was a man motivated by fear, Terra thought. He was afraid of Fenrir and had seen her battle the wolf in human form. He understood what she could do with him, especially without his ring to help him. She would use that.

"What do you know?"

"It was a heist. I worked with a few other people. No one knew what it was. We waited until he left the country and got past his security systems. All mechanical. Can you believe that? German thing, I guess. No lasers. No magnets. All clamps and gears. Must have been fun to build but easy to trick."

She stepped toward him. "I was asking about the ring."

"Right, yes! Sorry! We got into his safes, the rich bastard had multiple, and we took everything we could. The ring might have had documentation, I don't know. Lots of that sort of thing will, but I recognized solid gold for solid gold and slipped it on my finger."

"You stealing bastard," Mads snapped. "Put it on your

finger so you didn't have to count its value as part of the split. There's supposed to be honor among thieves."

"I regret it, I really do!" Marcus babbled. "If I had known half the trouble it would get me in, I would have tossed it out!"

"But you didn't," Terra stated.

"No, I can't say I did. It felt…right on my finger. Like it was supposed to be there. It felt perfect, and it was a simple enough thing. I figured I'd hold onto it and sell it one day if I got into a tight spot. But then I activated it."

"How?"

"It was another heist. This one in Spain? I think. Yes, Spain, because it was hot. The security in this place was top-notch, but I thought we had gotten past it all the same. I still think someone set us up because *la policia* were there *fast*. Had the place surrounded before we knew we'd been made. They busted in, and we all scrambled. Most of them tried to get out, but I tried to hide."

"By yourself, letting your teammates get hung up instead of you." Mads sneered.

"I didn't get into this line of work because I'm brave!" Marcus lamented. "I did it because I had no other choices. This was the only way to escape a childhood that—"

"What happened when you tried to hide?" Terra asked, cutting off the sob story. She had little doubt Marcus could cry on command and even less interest in seeing it.

"I hid behind a curtain by a window. Stupid, I know, but the light wasn't coming in behind me, and it was long enough to hide my feet. I thought it wasn't the worst thing ever. But it was. The *policia* came in and headed directly toward me. I didn't know what to do. There was nothing *to* do. I kept thinking if I were a fly on the wall, I'd be fine. A fly on the wall wouldn't be noticed. Then the ring began to glow."

Marcus smiled at the memory before continuing. "They opened the curtain and didn't see me at all. I was terrified, you understand, because they were so giant. It's odd being able to change forms, but you get used to it."

"We'll ask you for tips if we need them." Leif tossed the ring and caught it. Marcus hungrily watched it rise and fall.

He continued. "Before I knew what was happening, one of them winced and said something about a *mosca*. That's fly in Spanish, by the way. Then he tried to squish me! I got out of the way, only to realize I could fly! I tried to get out the window, but you have no idea how difficult it is to see glass when you're in the body of an insect. That probably saved my life. They saw me bounce against the window a few times and figured I was only a bug. They left, and I escaped a while later."

"Let me guess. You did *not* use your shapeshifting powers to help your team, who are all locked in a Spanish prison," Mads grated.

"I was going to. I really was! When I knew I could change into an insect, I naturally thought how I could use that power to save them."

"Naturally," Mads replied caustically.

"I wondered if a fly could accomplish all that, though. I could get into a jail, no problem, but how was I supposed to get three adults out? I decided to see what else the ring could do."

"Cue the training montage," Leif quipped.

Marcus grinned. "I wish I could have shortened it. At first, the only things I could become were a snake, which you all met, a biting fly, a salmon, and a horse."

"You mean a mare?" Leif corrected.

Marcus flushed. "How did you... I mean, what does the gender matter?"

"All those forms are associated with Loki. It is yet more proof this ring belongs to the trickster god."

"I don't know about all that," Marcus replied. "Only that the other forms took practice. I was focusing on the gorilla because I thought it would be most useful for helping my team out of jail. But I never got the chance to help them, much as I would have liked to."

"Fenrir found you," Terra stated.

"He did. I tried to fight him off. At this point, I thought I was pretty skilled as both the snake and the gorilla. But he was...well, you fought him. I could hardly scratch him, let alone stop him from beating me. He beat me within an inch of my life and forced me to serve him, so that's what I've been doing ever since."

'What else has he made you steal?" Terra questioned.

"He had me in North America to track down a scepter or a wand, something like that. Except someone apparently broke it. He became quite furious at that."

Terra and Mads glanced at Leif, who looked pleased with himself.

"What else?" Terra asked.

"It was only the wand thing. Then I was supposed to steal the box or whatever was in it from you. I didn't want to, you understand. Stealing from an active archeological site? I would never have done that. I value the, uh...work you archeologists do. I only steal things millionaires have taken out of the public eye. I'm a modern-day Robin Hood! Or I was until Fenrir stopped me."

"You're skipping the part where you tried to escape," Mads prompted.

Marcus glared at him. "What are you talking about?"

"Don't be a little shit. You've told us you're the sort of man who knows when it's time to escape. You're also a man who can turn into a fly. No one in their right mind would think you didn't try to run away from the bastard."

"I did try to escape. Twice. The first time, I only made it a few hours before he caught up to me. When he did, it was bad. I… He made me transform, then beat me so I could heal the wounds. I only tried once more. I lasted longer that time, but he still caught me all the same. It's not worth standing up to him. Now that he's after you, you need to accept that. He's unbelievably powerful. I can become a poisonous anaconda, and I still can't stop him."

"How did he find you?" Leif held the ring in the palm of his hand, staring at it instead of Marcus.

"I don't have a freaking clue," Marcus replied.

"Yes, you do," Mads insisted. "Or else you wouldn't have lasted longer the second time you tried to escape. What did you do differently?"

Marcus' eyes twitched to the ring in Leif's hand.

"You left the ring behind," Terra realized. "That's how you ducked him. You didn't have the ring."

Leif's eyes went wide as the circle of gold in his hand.

Mads grimaced and rested his hand on the gun tucked into his waistband.

"He still found me, though. He has a sense of smell like

you cannot believe. He's probably following all your scents right now."

"But the first time, it was the ring," Terra persisted.

Mads pulled out his gun and stuck it against Marcus' head. "This is a setup, isn't it? You came here to buy time for Fenrir to find us."

"No! I swear! That's not the sort of guy he is. Even if he wanted that, he wouldn't tell *me!* He treats me like garbage. He didn't say anything about following me or anything like that. He never even said he could track Loki's artifacts! He only said I needed to find you all and bring him the ax and the other things you have, or he'd beat me again!" The smell of urine wafted from the bound man. "Please! I would never!"

"Never what? Turn on the people who are holding you captive?" Mads shoved the barrel more firmly against Marcus' forehead.

"I didn't want to be a part of any of this. I was only trying to rob enough loot to spend a few months in Spain without worrying about getting a job. Please, you have to believe me!"

His words rang false when one of the cabin walls smashed in. Fenrir stood there, his massive shoulders framed against the setting sun outside.

Now that Terra knew his name, he was obviously the bound wolf. Even under his long black cloak, he rippled with an unnatural amount of muscle. The thick hair on the back of his neck seemed to rise and fall as he breathed. Those hideous, curving teeth would have looked completely natural in the face of a wolf.

"I knew it would not be long until we met again," Fenrir

growled. He stepped into the wreckage of the wall he'd destroyed.

"We knew you'd show up again, too, mate. You could have at least come in through one of the broken windows," Mads complained.

Fenrir growled. "Enough talk. Give me the items, or I will take them from you. You have no right."

"I guess you're going to have to take them, then," Terra countered. "Because the way I heard it, you're not supposed to be on Midgard at all."

"How dare you speak to a man with the blood of a god in his veins?" Fenrir snarled.

"I have that, too. It's not as rare as you'd think," Leif replied.

The Asgardian put the ring on his finger and shifted into the form of a massive serpent.

"Perhaps this fight will actually get my blood up." Fenrir growled.

Then, wolf and serpent crashed into each other.

CHAPTER FOURTEEN

Good Fun Cabin #3, Brissund, Gotland, Sweden, Thursday Afternoon

Since Leif came to Midgard, he had been growing steadily in power. He had not been able to tap into *seidr* in Asgard. He now assumed it was because he had always been overwhelmed by what those around him could do. Now, in Midgard, with the power of a cat's eyeball plucked from the Bygul who pulled Freya's chariot, Leif had tasted power. He had worn Freya's bracers, wielded the ax, and even used Brísingamen to teleport.

Yet he had never felt power like this.

It flowed from the ring into his bones. Unlike the invigorating power of the *seidr* from Freya's bracers, this magic could not be expressed into the world around him. He had to use it himself, in his own body. And it wanted him to be a snake.

"How dare you speak to a man with the blood of a god in his veins?" Fenrir snarled.

Leif looked at his jagged teeth and his massive shoulders. He knew he could not sense the power radiating off him because the amulet around his neck hid it. Still, this would not be an easy fight. It would be safer to stand down, cede the artifacts to Fenrir, and beg for his grandmother's help. If they believed Marcus' terrified rambling, he was not supposed to be here.

The gods might turn a blind eye to the happenings of mortals, but they were not so flippant about their own rules and proclamations.

"I have that, too. It's not as rare as you'd think," Leif replied. He did not know what compelled him to say that exactly. He had spent multiple mortal lifetimes arguing against the unnecessary use of force beings like Thor and Baldr employed so casually. Yet now, in this broken cabin on Midgard, the very idea of acquiescing to this brute's demands seemed repugnant.

Still, he was as surprised as anyone when he slipped the ring on his finger. He finally allowed its power to flow through him and shifted into a massive serpent.

"Perhaps this fight will actually get my blood up." Fenrir growled. It was the last thing Leif heard before his fangs sunk into Fenrir's shoulder.

Hot venom flowed through his fangs and into Fenrir's sinewy shoulder. Yet rather than triumph at having bitten their foe, Leif felt terror. Now that he was touching Fenrir, he could sense the power of the demigod he was trying to stop. He tried to constrict Fenrir, but before he could get a coil around him, pain coursed through his abdomen.

Fenrir had grabbed his serpent body and was crushing it in his hand like a jelly-filled donut.

Another spot of pain, then Leif was ripped free of

Fenrir and tossed across the room. He smashed into the sofa, toppling it backward. He'd had the wind knocked out of him, and he desperately tried to suck air. When he did, he shifted back into a human. Still trying to breathe, Leif focused on the fight.

Terra would not be intimidated, even if Fenrir had tossed an anaconda like an overcooked noodle.

She teleported in close enough to slice Fenrir across the chest with her ax, then teleported back. Fenrir crashed forward. She vanished, reappeared behind him, and slashed him in the back.

"Enough of these tickle attacks! Stop pretending to fight me and *fight* me!" Fenrir roared.

Yet Leif had trained Terra well. He emphasized the importance of control again and again. Terra did not rise to Fenrir's challenge but kept her distance. She spun Freya's ax in two quick loops and blasted a pair of energy darts at Fenrir. The first hit him in the face, and he swatted the second away.

Then he charged Terra. She didn't teleport away this time. Instead, she waited for the last moment. She ducked low, grabbed one of Fenrir's shoulders, and rammed her forearm into his waist above his hip. He toppled over her, a slave to his godly momentum, and crashed through the wall of the cabin to sprawl into the yard.

The roof buckled. A dusting of plaster rained down on them, but it held.

"I'm here, sir! I'm here!" Marcus pleaded, looking from the roof to Fenrir and back. He didn't seem entirely convinced Fenrir was less dangerous than a roof falling onto him, but the coward could not resist calling for help.

Leif reached into the power of the ring and felt for another form. After what Fenrir had done to him as a snake, he had little confidence in overpowering the wolf in human form. However, maybe he didn't need to focus on his entire body. One spot might do it.

Leif transformed into a fly. He had not fully anticipated how it would feel to be small enough to fit in the palm of his own hand. He was large for a fly, which was quite tiny for a battle with a demigod. Yet he was fast. All he had to do was think *there,* and the fly body responded, taking him where he wished to go with buzzing wings.

So he thought *Fenrir's ugly face* and zipped through the giant hole in the side of the cabin toward the hulking man. He buzzed in his face and landed on his eyebrow, then *bit.*

It was obviously not the body of a normal fly. A normal fly could not have split the flesh of a god who could withstand bullets. This was a piece of Loki and thus could do things that would have been impossible for a regular insect. Like bite through Fenrir's eyebrow with enough force to make the demigod's blood spurt and run into his eye.

Fenrir roared. Leif thought *escape* and buzzed away to hide on the cabin wall.

Terra saw the opportunity he had created and ran in the opposite direction, toward Fenrir instead of away. Her fist smashed into his face, and he stumbled backward from the force of it.

On the wall, Leif felt the remaining timbers rattle from the blow.

Terra knew it wouldn't be enough. As she completed the most massive punch she had ever delivered, she was already swinging the ax in her other hand at Fenrir's meaty thigh.

The ax landed with a wet *squelch* and stuck in his leg.

Before she could pull the blade back out, Fenrir grabbed her bracer.

"And I had thought the Asgardian would present the challenge," he growled. Then he *squeezed.*

Leif had no doubt Terra's bones would have been crushed to powder had she not worn the bracers. The rose gold armor was too strong for Fenrir, so instead, he used the grip to throw Terra into the cabin, directly at the spot where Leif was trying to be a fly on the wall.

Even with the speed of his wings, Leif could not get clear. Terra bashed into him. Leif hit his head and saw stars.

Then he felt Fenrir's crushing force on his wrist. His fingers unwrapped, unbidden, and Fenrir's claw-like hands dug into Leif's finger, pulling the ring off.

Its power was lost to Leif as Fenrir reclaimed his prize.

"Sir, please! Give me the ring, and I can help you!" Marcus pleaded. He was still duct-taped to the chair, though now he was on his side.

Leif would never know if Fenrir would have granted that wish because Terra was already behind the demigod, swinging her ax into the small of his back.

The blow hit true, and the power of Freya's ax knocked Fenrir forward. He stumbled and nearly fell but caught himself on the opposite wall, which again shook the structure. Leif did not think the cabin would last much longer.

Despite the blood, Fenrir did not look weakened, only angered. He turned to Terra, who only tightened her grip on her ax. Fenrir roared. The ring in his hand glowed, then the energy flowed into him. It did not make him change form, though. It only seemed to make the muscles on his neck bulge more impressively.

He loosed another roar and charged at Terra. She teleported out of the way and tried to slash his back, but Fenrir was ready for her. He dodged the strike and got between her and the weapon, grabbed her by the throat, and slammed her into the ceiling.

Her shoulders smashed through the crumbling plaster, and her head struck a beam. She went limp as she lost consciousness. Freya's ax fell from her hand.

Fenrir hardly noticed, enraged as he was. He smashed her into the ceiling again and again. Finally, the beam gave way, and Terra flew into the sky.

The cabin sagged but somehow stayed up.

"The ax, mate," Mads panted, then slunk past Leif and out of the house, following Terra's trajectory.

Leif hated that Mads was right. They couldn't let Fenrir get the ax. He was distracted chasing after Terra, and Mads would help with that. Leif had to get the ax.

So, instead of going to his friend, he retrieved the weapon he was supposed to somehow use to save her life. He picked it up and felt energized. He could do this. He *had* to do this.

Leif gritted his teeth and charged out of the cabin at Fenrir.

He fired a blast from the ax that hit Fenrir just before he scooped Terra up.

The demigod grunted and turned to Leif with fury in

his eyes, which were now tinged yellow, like the wolf he truly was.

Mads chose that moment to shoot the bastard several times in the chest.

Fenrir roared, though the bullets hardly did a thing to him. His chest dimpled where he had been hit, but only one bullet punched through. It was a waste of ammunition...except Leif realized what Mads was doing. He was aiming for the amulet. That was their shot. Hit the amulet and destroy Fenrir's tether to the magic he needed in this realm.

Leif could work toward that. He couldn't overpower Fenrir, but he could damage his jewelry. He shot two more ax blasts that Fenrir swiped away. However, they let Leif get close enough to swipe at his head, then his legs. When Fenrir blocked each blow with a forearm, Leif reached his other hand for the amulet around the man's neck.

Only to get backhanded across the face and sent flying.

Leif felt something smash into his back, then everything went dark except a single spot of light. His brain struggled to make sense of what he was seeing, only to realize he was back in the cabin. Fenrir had bashed him through the wall with a single blow. Through the hole, he saw Fenrir stomping toward him.

Behind him, Terra still lay unconscious. Leif glimpsed Mads, rushing toward Terra before Fenrir reached the cabin and threw a shoulder into it.

The wall fared no better than the pine tree had. It crashed inward, and the entire roof sagged. Fenrir grinned at Leif, spat, then marched back toward Terra.

Leif didn't see anything more after that because the entire side of the house collapsed.

He scrambled backward, trying to get clear before the rest of the roof came down on him. He was still dazed and was nowhere near a door, only cracks in the walls and broken windows.

Then Mads appeared in a crack of energy and laid a hand on Leif. Together, they teleported outside the cabin.

If it were up to Leif, he would have gone a bit farther.

Mads got them clear, but only by a few feet. When the cabin collapsed, a spray of debris and dust caught them. Leif wanted to move away from the noise, but Mads didn't let him. He pushed him to the ground with his body and hissed in his face.

"I say, try to show some class,"

"We can't let him hear us. Now, shush," Mads insisted.

From the other side of the cabin, Fenrir howled. Then came a thrashing noise that faded. He had retreated. For now.

"We have to save her," Leif sobbed. "He'll rip her to pieces."

It suddenly occurred to him that Mads should not have been the one teleporting them to safety.

"I don't know, mate. If he wanted to do that, I think he could have. He was trying to pry off her bracers. I don't know if it's about her or the artifacts, but I'm hoping it's the objects." He held up his hand, and Leif saw Brísingamen clutched between his fingers.

"That's what you were doing? Poor Terra was knocked out cold, and you were using the opportunity to rob her?"

"Don't be a prick, mate. If I hadn't taken this, Fenrir

would have it now. We couldn't have that. At least this way, we have two artifacts instead of zero. And we can find Terra with that map of yours, can't we?"

"I suppose we can, yes. We'll have to act quickly. There's no way to know what he wants with her."

The wreckage of the cabin shifted, and a face covered in dust and dirt appeared.

"Actually, mate, there might be a way," Mads stomped toward where Marcus had poked out. The fool didn't try to run, as he was too snagged in the destruction of the house to do that. Instead, he tried to burrow back down inside.

Mads leveled a gun at him before he could fully vanish, which stopped him quickly.

"Can't crawl away like a rat, eh, mate? Might as well come and talk to us. At this range, I can shoot you a couple of times without killing you."

"Why does everyone resort to bullying?" Marcus forced a laugh. "I *want* to help you. Really!"

"Climb out of the pile and start talking."

"I want to. That's exactly what I want to do!" Marcus exclaimed.

Leif couldn't be sure, but he felt like he saw the thief try to change shape at least twice before coming to terms with the fact that his boss had the ring and he wouldn't get it back anytime soon.

"What's that bastard want with Terra?" Mads asked.

"He wants Freya's artifacts. That's it!"

"Well, we have those. Does that mean he's coming for us?" Leif asked.

"He's got two of his own now. He'll want to use those. If

Terra can help him, he'll be pleased. He won't hurt her if she helps him."

"Help him with what?" Leif asked.

"The box I retrieved for him. How to open it has eluded him. My master is many things but is not known for his puzzle-solving skills."

"You seem like the puzzle-solving sort. You couldn't figure it out either?" Mads asked.

"I tried my best, I really did, but no. I, uh, I couldn't figure it out."

"Why does he want the artifacts?" Leif pressed. "What good are they?"

"He is limited in power here. Even I know that much. He wants them to grow stronger."

"What does he want with strength, though? If all he craves is power, he could have stayed in Niflheim. He should not have been diminished there like he is on Midgard. It's closer on the world tree to the primordial power."

"I don't know anything primordial anything!" Marcus whined. "I know he didn't like it there. He would threaten to banish me there if I didn't do as he said."

"But he has enough power to survive on Midgard, doesn't he?" Mads asked Leif.

"I suppose he should. It will take time for him to recharge himself between these bouts, but much like the power that fills Terra's bracers, it should replenish."

"So why's he making a splash?" Mads demanded of Marcus.

"He's not trying to make a splash. He doesn't care about Midgard. He's said that enough times. He thinks it stinks here, and it's too loud. I don't think he wants to conquer this place if that's what you're thinking."

"I want to know what *you're* thinking, mate. Why go for the artifacts when it's drawing so much attention?" Mads questioned.

"Because it's attention he's after," Leif mused, thinking it through. "He doesn't care about Midgard, or Asgard for that matter. He wants Loki."

Marcus flinched at the name.

"That's right, then?" Mads prodded.

Marcus was shaking now. "If he really is what you say he is, he's a *god,*" Marcus stammered.

"A demigod, technically, but yes."

"He doesn't tell me his wishes. I'm beneath him. He's made that very clear. He uses me because I had a piece of his father. That's all."

"That's what drives him, then? His dead old da?"

"I don't know. Like I said, he doesn't tell me these things, but he does speak of Loki. I don't know if he wants to hurt him, help him, or only find him, but he talked about him. It's *all* he talked about. He doesn't care about Terra. He doesn't even care about these artifacts. Not really. All he cares about is using them to get what he wants. He won't kill her. Not if he thinks she can help him get into that box."

"And if she cracks it and lets him in?"

"Then he'll be done with her and come after the two of you for the other artifacts."

CHAPTER FIFTEEN

<u>A lake, Gotland, Sweden, dawn</u>

Terra struggled for air. She swam toward the surface, feeling her lungs burn as she kicked and kicked through seaweed, tangling her and pulling her down. She burst through the water of the icy lake, but she still could not breathe. She had given herself the ability to breathe underwater, but it had come too late. Now she was on the surface, only to need water to breathe.

She grabbed at her neck, feeling for Brísingamen, and found it wasn't there. Her teleportation powers were further out of reach. She tried to cut the seaweed that pulled at her legs with Freya's ax, but it was gone, too. She could only feel Freya's bracers on her wrists, but they were growing heavier. Colder. Blocks of ice made it so her arms couldn't move, couldn't swim. Then the ice was sinking, pulling her back underwater. Into the biting cold. Into the dark. Too cold. Too dark. It was all fading. Slipping away. Over.

Then her cheek burned with pain, and she snapped awake.

She was on the ground in a cave. Fenrir towered over her. His jagged teeth were slightly parted, dousing her in stinky doggy breath. His eyes glowed yellow in the torchlight.

"Your heart stopped for a moment there." Fenrir sounded like an archeologist examining a shard of pottery. "I started it again."

He stood and walked away from Terra, his back to her, exposed. Terra wanted to attack, even if she didn't have her ax, but the thought sent shudders of exhaustion through her body. She could hardly breathe. The air felt thick and heavy.

"What did you do to me?" Terra tried to demand, but it emerged a whimper.

"The bracers on your wrists are stubborn. I want their power. They would not open. So I'll take it from you."

"Is that what you want from me?" Terra asked. "You're going to feed off me? I thought using a mortal like that would be beneath someone of your stature."

Fenrir snarled at that. Maybe she deserved it. It was probably not wise to antagonize him. Especially not now. Terra felt her *seidr* trickling back, but she was almost empty. She wouldn't be able to do a thing to him as long as she was like this. She needed time to replenish. Which meant she had to get him talking.

"I guess I'm relieved that I'm still alive," Terra stated.

Fenrir grunted. An acknowledgment of something, but what?

"You are not strong. You are only using power that is not yours."

Terra could not exactly argue. She was drained and lacking part of her arsenal. If he wanted power, the ax would have been a better prize.

"But you are clever. Are you not?" Fenrir asked.

"What makes you say that?" It might be dangerous to be anything except direct with Fenrir, but she needed to know what he knew. How long had he been in Midgard? How much did he understand?

He pointed to her bracers. "Those were locked up as well."

"They were in a box. That's correct."

"And you opened it."

"I did."

"See? Clever. Very clever. Now, you will work for me."

He approached a pile of all sorts of things. Viking swords, silver coins, broken chains. Some of the weapons were from different eras. Centuries of treasures thrown together in a midden pile in a cave. She knew that any archeologist worth tenure could sort it all out, but it bothered her to see so much history all tossed together like nothing more than trash.

Fenrir pulled the box from the pile and tossed it to Terra. She tried to catch it, but even that was beyond her current capabilities. The best she could do was fumble and catch it on her legs instead of letting it hit the ground.

"You are weak," Fenrir stated. It was not a question but a comment. He sniffed at her. Terra felt strangely violated when he did it. Like he could sense things others could not.

Her scent, yes, but also her feelings. "There is more power in the bracers."

"But you couldn't take them," Terra pointed out.

"I could not remove them," Fenrir flexed his fingers.

"Why? You don't need the strength they grant."

"No," Fenrir admitted, showing his fearsome teeth. "I am strong enough thanks to the magic I have from you. But with more magic, I could fight until the end of time."

Still bruised and battered from their last bout, Terra didn't think the monstrous wolf in the body of a man needed any more stamina or anything else. He was a powerhouse looking to become dauntless. She could not let it come to pass, but how was she supposed to stop it?

"So you're not after the skills these artifacts grant?" She didn't know where Brísingamen was, only that it wasn't around her neck. The idea of a brute like Fenrir with the ability to teleport was a terrifying thought.

"I wish only my own strength. If I can use the power of Niflheim I had in Asgard, I will no longer be so weak." Fenrir smiled.

A terrifying thought, Fenrir believed knocking through a few trees or leveling a cabin was not true strength.

"Surely there are other ways to achieve those goals. These objects belong to Freya. Why not seek out the artifacts of your father?"

Fenrir's easy grin turned into a vicious thing. "My father is a rat. He dealt with those lying Asgardians and trapped me. I do not trust his power."

"Is that why you used the ring for strength instead of to change shape?"

"I don't need *strength*," Fenrir growled, cords of muscle

standing out on his neck. "I am strong. Stronger than any of the gods. I have killed Odin and taken the hand of Tyr. I will kill others, and they will tremble at what they did to me. They will wish they killed me. My father will see his deception for cowardice when I find him."

"And you're sure your father doesn't know where you are right now? Perhaps he is already watching your actions."

"I don't think so," Fenrir replied. Terra didn't think he meant to, but one of his clawed hands drifted to the amulet around his neck. "He will look for me and only find me when it is too late. I will have enough power then. Enough power to make them all answer for what they have done. And you will give it to me. Open the box, *now!*"

"Sure. Do you know what's inside it, though? I'm only wondering if it's raw power you want, other artifacts might grant—"

"I will take your bracers from your corpse if you do not open the box. Now, cease this blather and open it."

"Right." Terra turned her attention to the box in her hands. She tried to focus on the puzzle as she turned the object over and over, but her mind kept returning to how she might get out of here.

Was it possible? Right now, she was so weak the idea of escape was laughable. Furthermore, she had no idea where she was other than underground. She might be able to save up enough *seidr* to teleport away, but where would she go?

She needed a specific place. She couldn't go back to the cabin since it was destroyed. Teleporting from one cave across who knew how many miles to a room in another was not something she wished to attempt. Maybe if she had full power, but in this state, she'd probably run out halfway through and end up part of a future archeological discovery.

"What do you see?" Fenrir demanded.

That did not leave much for puzzling about her future. She focused on the box, looking for some clue to open it.

Almost immediately, she saw it.

Her thumb pushed a piece on the back of the box. It turned out the back was not actually solid but a collection of tiny tiles that could be moved. She didn't dare move one in front of Fenrir. Instead, she turned the box again and pored over the delicate runes carved into its surface.

"Perhaps you are not as clever as I had hoped," Fenrir growled.

"There's something here in the runes." Terra pointed to the delicate inscriptions on the golden lid. "Something about…let's see. To find my contents, you must know my contents. Only the worthy with knowledge of their future may unlock the present."

"Asgardian nonsense," Fenrir snapped.

"Maybe, maybe not." Terra swallowed, not sure what to do. She turned the box again and looked at the back, finding what she thought. It was the feathered cloak. It looked like tool marks in its current configuration, but Terra could make out the edges where it was supposed to wrap around the wearer's neck. It would take a few minutes to move the pieces into the right spaces, but not much longer.

And Fenrir was staring right at her. "Is there a hidden catch?"

"No. I don't think so," Terra answered too quickly, but

Fenrir did not seem to notice. He was probably accustomed to terrifying people with his presence, considering even the gods feared Fenrir Wolf.

"Then how does it open?"

"I think we need to know what's inside. I think it might be the cloak. Her feathered cloak. Have you seen it?" Maybe it was a mistake to tell him the cloak was inside, but it was not an artifact associated with strength. He could lose interest.

"Excellent. You are very clever. Open it quickly, and I can drink from its power. It was always prized. It will give me strength for weeks."

Terra did not know if he was exaggerating or merely being hopeful, but even if the cloak granted him the level of strength he had for days instead of hours, he would be an unstoppable force on this planet. Maybe a tank, or certainly a nuke, could bring him down. Short of that, Terra didn't see any way to stop him.

Only she could. She could not open the box and give him the contents. Yet she had the solution in front of her, and Fenrir did not seem like he had anything more important to do than watch her grant him the key to limitless strength.

"When you have this, you'll be done?" Terra asked.

"When I have the cloak, I will decide how much of my time you have wasted. You will decide whether you are going to take those bracers off or if I should bite off your arms like I did Tyr."

Not exactly the easiest environment in which to stall.

CHAPTER SIXTEEN

Road 149, Northbound, Gotland, Sweden, Thursday evening

"Mate, I'm not saying you're wrong. I'm only saying he covered a lot of ground rather quickly," Mads stated. He was driving to the northern tip of Gotland, following Leif's magic map like their lives depended on it. Though, if Leif's assessment of the situation was correct, the lives of everyone on the island might be at stake.

"We did not see him wither this time, which means he left with something of his strength intact. Marcus, tell us, have you seen him move at great speeds?"

Mads didn't like bringing the former shapeshifter with them, but he didn't have any plans that the shifty, spineless twerp wouldn't improve. There was the chance they would show up, and Marcus would sing like a canary and foil their entire plan, but they were betting against that.

"He can lope like a wolf. He keeps running and running. He doesn't need a car to get where he wants to go," Marcus whimpered. The bloke was terrified of Fenrir, which was the only reason Mads had agreed to keep him on. Marcus had been questioning his place in the world, and maybe his sanity, since discovering that not only could he change shape but that a man who styled himself Fenrir wanted him to use that power to steal ancient relics.

Discovering Fenrir was not the only person in the world with powers like that seemed to have flipped a switch in Marcus' brain. He saw Leif and Mads as his chance to get out from underneath Fenrir's brutal rule. It might be a long shot, but it was his only shot. They would use that, mostly because they had no other choice.

"See? The map works. I'm quite familiar with Terra's particular magical signature, and it's keyed into the map. I don't think Fenrir is deceiving us with false magic."

"Oh, he's not doing that," Marcus agreed from the back seat. His wrists and ankles were tied, which Mads believed was the only reason he had not dived out of the car.

"Explain," Mads demanded.

"He doesn't deceive. He doesn't trick. He never understood how changing shape could be useful. He always thought I could turn into a brute like him and hurt people but never really understood how a smaller form could be more effective."

"What about the amulet around his neck?" Leif asked. "That's a deception. It keeps him from being seen."

Marcus laughed from the back seat. "You think I would dare *ask* him why he wears that medallion?" He chuckled. "I would not guess at the will of a being like Fenrir Wolf."

"That's what it does, mate. Why would he use it if he doesn't like tricks?"

"Because he knows he's not at his full strength. He

complains about that constantly. He doesn't want to be seen until he's strong enough to return to Asgard. If he can do *that,* there will be no stopping him. What do I have to say to make you two idiots see that? We *cannot* stop him. He's not like us. Not even like you with your illusions." Marcus sneered at Leif. "He's beyond us. Unbelievably powerful."

"And you wish to run from that your entire life? You wish to eke out your mortal existence constantly looking over your shoulder, searching for threats?"

Marcus shrugged. "I'm a professional thief. That's pretty much how I live already."

"It is not, mate, and you know it," Mads countered. "I've been where you are. The world is stacked against you, so you might as well pinch a few crumbs, right?"

"Knowing that they might catch us, yeah."

"Catch you, mate. *Catch. You.* That's my point. You always know as long as you're careful, the worst thing that's going to happen is some agent catching up to you, and you'll end up in jail with three square meals a day and plenty of free time. That doesn't scare a bloke like you. Otherwise, you wouldn't be thieving. This is different, though, innit? This is the end of you. The hairy bastard would probably eat you if he could."

"Why do you think I'm even here?" Marcus snapped. "I don't think this will work, but if there's a chance I can get my ring back and make the giant wolf monster stop hunting me down, I'll try it."

Mads' hands tightened on the steering wheel, and he made them relax. He might not have respected Marcus, but he understood where he was coming from. Even cowards had to choose which of two options was less terrifying. Marcus was throwing in with them, at least for now. Mads didn't trust the little weasel, but he had faith Marcus would try to get his ring if there was any chance they could stop Fenrir. Mads had worked bigger jobs with less confidence. They could make it work.

If only he knew what *it* was.

"I'm still not seeing how we're going to stand against the big bad wolf," Mads told Leif. "I know I have the torc, and you have the ax, but Terra's better with both than we are. Not seeing how we have any chance of overpowering him when she had those plus her bracers and still lost.

"My hope is we will not personally contend with Fenrir. I'm sure you've heard the legends that Heimdall is always watching. Well, if we reveal a giant wolf crashing around Midgard, he will see."

"How do we do that, exactly? Can't you reach out to your great-grandmum?"

"Unfortunately, cellular phones do not exist in Asgard. We must do all we can to remove the amulet and get Heimdall's attention."

"Shite, mate. I was worried you'd say that. I tried, you know. Shot at the damn thing and missed. If we want to take it off, we might have to get closer."

"You understand this is a bad plan, right? It's a very bad plan. Let's take a day to figure out something better," Marcus interjected.

"It certainly makes more sense than us trying to beat him into submission. If the gods could not do that, we will not be able to come close, even if he is weakened on Midgard."

"And you're sure they'll send someone for him?" Mads asked. "No offense to your kin, but they're not exactly the most available."

"Fenrir will draw their attention. Ever since he appeared in Asgard, the Vanir and Aesir have been aware of his terrible strength. Even before Ragnarök, they recognized him as a threat. When he killed Odin—well, it was not as if they thought him weaker. If he escaped from his prison, someone is looking for him. All we need to do is draw their eye."

"Unless someone *let* him out," Marcus rejoined. "If that's the case, you might be taking away the only thing keeping him under control."

"I do not think that will be the case. You said he is searching for Loki, and I can think of no other god who would go through such subterfuge with Fenrir. Besides, the gods would not trust Loki to guard Fenrir. It would be too large a temptation. I feel certain if we can remove or destroy the medallion, we will not be left to fight him ourselves."

"Pop the necklace, and we win the match? Sounds too good to be true, mate. Not gonna lie on that," Mads insisted.

"He will not be immediately banished to another realm. It will take time for them to notice him, especially if he exercises control. Then it will take more time for them to arrive. We will have to fend him off for a bit, but what other choice do we have?"

"I don't see other options. Not if we want Terra alive, and I think we do," Mads agreed.

"That's my feeling on the matter as well. So drive onward and turn ahead. I believe we are close."

"Still not sure how much help I'm going to be," Marcus moaned from the back seat. "If your plan is really to take the only thing keeping him from becoming a monster, could you do me a favor and throw me out of the car? I'd rather take my chances with that."

CHAPTER SEVENTEEN

<u>A cave, Gotland, Sweden</u>

Terra had already wasted an hour fiddling around with the box. She didn't see how she could waste another.

"You said the pieces on the back move. How hard can it be to move them into the right sequence? Can you not read the runes?"

"I can, but I can't figure out what they mean."

It was a stroke of luck that Fenrir could not actually read. It seemed literacy was still viewed as a privilege in Asgard, and the mad dog son of Loki and a giant did not pass the grade for being taught to read. Terra had convinced him the marks on the moving pieces were a message, not an image, and he had not figured out her deception. If he had, she wouldn't be alive anymore.

"There was a mosaic in the cave, and you were in it. Do you know why that would be?" Terra asked.

"A mosaic?" Fenrir tried out the word in his mouth of jagged teeth.

"An image made of little pieces of stone. Like a painting.

It was an altar to Freya, yet you and your siblings were pictured. Do you know why that would be? It might be important."

"Maybe it is simply that the cowards fear us. They always stayed behind their walls in their shining city. They kept out my mother's people. Banished my sister. Tossed my brother into the ocean. They cared only for themselves. I am not surprised they would make images of us. They fear us, but they are wise. They do not face their fears but trick them."

Nothing but bitter hate there, Terra thought. She had to try another tactic. "What about the contents of the box? Could there be some meaning there?"

"I don't *care* what's in the box. I only want the power. Then I can unleash more of my strength upon this world."

"Because you wish to reunite with your father and rule this place with him?"

"Never!" Fenrir snarled and stomped toward her. He only stopped when she held up the box between them. He snarled at it, at her, at everything.

"You *don't* wish to reunite with your father?"

"I wish to kill him. I wish to rip his leg off and watch him shift into another form, then rip a leg off that as well. Again and again and again."

"Because of what happened after Ragnarök?" Terra pressed. The topic obviously infuriated Fenrir, yet Terra could not help her curiosity. She was already at the mercy of the wolf in human form. She might as well learn more about him if she could.

"Yes! But more than that. Even before Ragnarök, he abandoned us. He did not stop them from throwing my brother into the ocean. He never came to see me when I was bound in Gleipnir."

"Perhaps he could not risk the other gods seeing him go to you," Terra suggested.

"Pah! That is cowardly. If he is so scared, he is no father of mine. He could have come in one of his disguises, and none of the others would have noticed. All they care about is meat and mead. They don't even share their scraps with us. We are beneath them, and Loki used us to push himself up. He only bedded my mother to make monsters for children. He doesn't care about us. Only the chaos we created."

"So you don't think he helped you escape, then?" Terra asked. She didn't know how Fenrir got out of Niflheim but thought it would be good to find out. If he was sent back there, the gods would need to make sure he didn't get out again the same way. Loki helping him escape was the only thing that Terra could think of. Fenrir had confirmed what the myths had always claimed. The gods were afraid of him. They would not have freed him on purpose.

"I only escaped because my guard found a cask of mead. He drank his fill and fell asleep on a branch of the world tree. I ran from his sight and found another root he should have destroyed. I climbed onto the branches of the world tree."

"And you were able to navigate to Midgard? That is impressive. I've read the tangles of Yggdrasil are such that even the gods become lost."

Fenrir smiled. "I could smell the stench of Midgard. In its reek, I detected the essence of my father. I knew Asgard would be protected from my approach, but if I could find pieces of my father on Midgard, perhaps I could deceive them.

"Still, I could not find my way. The branches of Yggdrasil are large. They double back and twist on themselves. I became lost. Then, it was not so hard once Ratatoskr came to me. He thought to fill my head with lies and false paths. I let him lead me for a time. Then, when he thought I was wrapped in his webs, I took his tail in my jaws."

"Wait. He has a tail?"

"Of course Ratatoskr has a tail! He is a squirrel!" Fenrir growled. "Which you should know. You have studied the myths. You know much of the other realms for a mortal."

"I have studied the legends, Lord Fenrir, that is true. But some parts are untrue. I did not know, for example, that you could take the form of a human. I thought your wolf body was the only one that could contain your power."

Fenrir's throat rumbled. "I cannot take this form without the power of the dwarfs."

"Ah. Of course." Terra bowed. "So the legends are true? Ratatoskr really is a squirrel?"

"More like a rat, but yes. He has always lived on the world tree. I do not think the mind of something in the body of a human could navigate its branches. This body is frail. Even the Aesir wear clothes to protect them from the cold or the heat. This body could not understand the branches of the world tree. It only understands the dirt and how it must build upon it or be returned to it."

"Yet you were able to trick Ratatoskr in his own realm? That could not have been easy."

"It was no trick. I do not deal in deceptions. Wearing this body irks me."

"Then how?"

"He grew confident and let me grow close. I took his tail in my jaws and told him to take me to Nidavellir."

"The realm of the dwarfs."

"Quite. I told them I would kill Ratatoskr unless they fashioned me something that would allow me to travel to Midgard. Ratatoskr helped convince them of my seriousness. I think the fur on his tail will grow back, but I cannot say." Fenrir sniggered at the memory.

"And from there, you had Ratatoskr lead you here."

"It was simple enough from Nidavellir. By then, Ratatoskr was desperate to be free of me."

"You were not concerned about finding your father had a Chosen on Midgard?"

Fenrir snorted. "Loki has no need of a champion on Midgard. He detests the very idea of such things. He strikes from the shadows, not the battlefield."

"But he left pieces of himself here as well. Do you know why?"

"Loki would not litter Midgard with his treasures for no purpose. I know that. He has a plan. He always has a plan, but it does not involve me. It has never involved me. I was an embarrassment to him, and my only purpose was to bite the hand of a god and kill another. None of this matters! You are supposed to open the box. Now, open it!"

"Let me look at the runes again. Now that I know your story—"

"My story has nothing to do with that box. That bitch Freya does not know I escaped. She does not know how I moved through the branches of the World Tree. You are wasting my time. Open the box now, or I will take your throat in my jaws and *make* you open it!"

"I'm trying, I really am!" Terra fiddled with the tiles, moving them back and forth, always careful to avoid forming the shape she already had in her mind. "I only wished to know if you and your siblings might have some significance. This mark here is the mark for Jotunn, I think. Maybe if I put it near the mark for trapped—"

"Enough of this! You have opened other boxes like this one. Do not dawdle!"

"Some of those boxes took days to open. Maybe if you could let me go to the surface and look at the box in the light, it would be clear to me."

"If I have to wait until dawn to open this box, I will do it myself. Your bracers will not come off, but I wonder if that will hold if I eat your heart."

"You know you can't force this open. Please, I want to help, but I can't think if you threaten my life!"

"A finger, then." Fenrir licked his lips. "Everyone on Midgard has all their fingers in this age. You do not need them. I will eat a finger, then another. Then you will open the box for me, and you will get to keep your heart."

Fenrir's ears pricked like a dog who'd heard the mailman.

Terra heard it a moment later. It was the mewling voice of Marcus, calling for Fenrir.

"Master! Master, I have recovered a piece of Freya!"

CHAPTER EIGHTEEN

<u>A cave on the North Coast, Gotland, Sweden, Thursday Night</u>

Marcus was smarter than this. He had to be smarter than this. He had taken gems from royals and stacks of hundred-dollar bills from safes in millionaires' homes. You could not be a thief and be dumb. Or you couldn't be a thief for long, anyway.

So he felt profoundly stupid, walking into Fenrir's lair with nothing but a scrap of lightly enchanted leather in his hands. Fenrir could snap him in half. Hell, Marcus would be *lucky* if that was all Fenrir did to him. The man was cruelty incarnate. He would have killed Marcus a dozen times over if not for the ring that made him useful to the sharp-toothed thug, who was also apparently a demigod.

A demigod Marcus was currently trying to deceive.

Did Mads and Leif not understand the profound stupidity of such a plan? If Fenrir saw through their deception, they would all be dead. Worse than dead. Fenrir would tear them to pieces. They would watch as he drank their blood.

Yet, what other choice did Marcus have? He had never asked for the magic ring. He never understood what it was. He had known it was magic. No technology could transform a body. If it did exist, it would almost certainly be some walk-in chamber with swirling mists pouring from the smoothly opening doors he stumbled upon in the basement of a millionaire he was trying to rob. His ring was beyond that.

But it wasn't his. According to Leif, it was the ring of a god, and Marcus had been its master. He didn't know what that meant. He didn't think he was destined for anything besides the beaches of some island. All he knew was the ring had given him the freedom he'd always craved.

With it, he didn't need to work with other thieves. He didn't need to spend months planning jobs. He could take whatever shape he needed, grab what he wanted, and leave. And he'd been getting better with it. He had learned more than animals. He could combine them or even wear the faces of other people. If he could master those skills, he would truly have freedom.

Except he couldn't. Not as long as Fenrir was around.

Fenrir could sense the ring.

If he really was a wolf, he could probably smell it.

As long as Fenrir was free, Marcus wouldn't be. Marcus hated it, but the simple truth was it was either him or the cruel demigod. He understood he was risking his life by agreeing to work against Fenrir, but a life spent as Fenrir's servant would be no life at all.

So he walked into the cave and forced himself to call out to the person he least wanted to see.

"Master! Master, I have recovered a piece of Freya!"

It was a lie, and a bad one, but it might buy them a few minutes. Hopefully, that was all they would need. Fenrir did not seem to understand Freya's artifacts like he did Loki's. He had not wielded the power of the ax and instead had Marcus do it.

"Marcus?" Fenrir's voice echoed through the cave.

Marcus drew a deep breath. At least now, Leif and Mads would not kill him. After it became clear that their map really was leading them to Terra and they would not be dissuaded from saving her, Marcus agreed to show them the entrance. He'd agreed to this charade. By calling Fenrir, he'd removed two threats to his life.

Too bad Fenrir felt like a hundred more.

"It is me, master! I lacked the strength to follow without the ring, but I found something in the wreckage." Marcus forced himself to walk deeper into the cave, hating every step. At least it was night, and the darkness of the cave was no more fearsome than the night itself. Marcus especially hated entering the cave in the daytime, when it felt like he was leaving the safety of the sun behind and entering the underworld. Right now, it felt like going from one part of hell to another.

"The torc? She does not have it. I do not know when she removed it," Fenrir stated, coming into view. He had no torch, no flashlight. He could see in the dark as well as Marcus when he was in the shape of a rat.

Marcus had a flashlight in one hand and the map in the other. He heard Fenrir's footsteps in the dark. He knew there would be light farther in. He himself had shown Fenrir how to use electric lights for his lair, but he did not want to go deep enough into the cave to see it. He kept walking, however.

"No. It is a marvel. A map that seems to show whatever the bearer wishes to see!"

Right now, Leif and Mads were using their own magic to turn themselves invisible and sneak past Fenrir. This was the most critical part of the entire mission. If Fenrir caught them *now*, he would surely blame Marcus for their incursion. If he did not catch them for a few minutes, he might think Marcus had been tricked. That was the angle Marcus would try to play.

For now, he wanted his freedom and believed only a god could truly stop Fenrir. So, despite his shaking hand, he raised the flashlight's beam and pointed it into Fenrir's eyes.

"Stop that, you fool!" Fenrir growled as his yellow eyes shrank to tiny pricks.

"Sorry, master! I apologize. I was only trying to help!"

"Give me the artifact." Fenrir drew close enough to Marcus that there would be no escape.

Marcus handed him the map, then shone the flashlight upon it.

"It was brave of you to return," Fenrir rumbled. "Did you come to serve me, or did you simply crave your ring?"

"Master, I live to serve. But of course if you would grant me the privilege of wearing the ring again, I would use it to achieve whatever you wish."

Fenrir laughed and thumped Marcus on the back with a heavy hand. "You are honest enough for me, Marcus. Of course you came for the ring. Perhaps, after I open the box, I will reward you with its return."

"You are too kind, master."

"Servants must be rewarded. My father never understood this. Though it must be said, you stink of the woman's allies." Fenrir sniffed distastefully, and for a terrible moment, Marcus thought it was all over. Surely, Fenrir would notice the smell was not coming from Marcus but from the cloaked infiltrators.

"I thought we could use this, master."

"What is this?" Fenrir looked at the moving lines of ink on the surface, then furrowed his brow. "I sense no great well of magic."

"I do not think it is supposed to be a thing of power but a tool. Do you see where it shows Terra on the map? If she escapes again, she will not be able to elude us."

"This is a map?" No recognition registered in Fenrir's eyes. No understanding at all. Leif and Mads had been concerned that Fenrir might see through their illusion and somehow make them appear on the map, but it turned out the mighty wolf did not even understand what he was looking at.

For the first time, Marcus actually felt bad for the demigod. Fenrir had spent his entire existence imprisoned. He didn't even know what a map was. It sounded like a cruel life. It was a shame he would be forced to return to it, but not so much that Marcus would try to prevent it. It was not his place to undo the cruelty done to Fenrir. Apparently, that responsibility lay with his father and the pantheon of Norse gods.

Yet all the pity in the world wouldn't stop Fenrir from ripping Marcus in half if he was displeased.

"This is the island of Gotland, as seen from above. It can also look closer." Marcus touched the map, and the image zoomed in with a splash of ink. Fenrir recognized the magic of that, at least. "With it, we can track down beings of magic."

"Can it show me the whereabouts of my father?"

"I cannot say, Lord Fenrir. Perhaps if you give me his ring, we can use its magic to make the map reveal him to us."

Fenrir snorted again. Marcus thought it might have been with displeasure. He would assume it was displeasure. That was the safest thing to assume with Fenrir.

"You stink, Marcus. How long did they have you bound?"

"Not long, my lord. I was able to escape when you destroyed their hovel, but I stuck around and stole this map when they grew distracted with your power."

Fenrir nodded, seemingly mollified. He brought the map closer to his face and inhaled deeply. When he did, the ink faded, and the leather seemed to dry out, but Fenrir did not seem pleased with this magical snack.

"There is hardly anything here. This will allow me no more time."

"Are you certain, my lord? I think it could be useful."

"Useful would be the ax or the gold she wears around her neck. Those have the power of Freya! This is nothing but a trick."

"It's not a trick, my lord. I swear it!" Marcus yelped much too loudly.

Fenrir narrowed his eyes. "I am surprised to see you back, Marcus. Without the ring, you might have escaped my notice."

"My lord, I cannot go back to such an existence. I lived my entire life in ignorance, not knowing the powers that exist in this world. I don't want to go back to that. I would rather serve you, my lord. If you would but give me the ring, I am sure we could use this map to find where on the island they are hiding from you."

Fenrir chuckled. "I should have known you came back for your trinket. You are clever enough to see that you are better with me. Come. We will cut off this girl's hands, and the bracers will be mine."

A cave on the North Coast, Gotland, Sweden, Thursday night

Mads didn't like being invisible. He realized as a professional thief, he should have embraced this most sneaky of abilities. Maybe he would have if he'd been the one actually creating the magical effect. Having to rely on the Asgardian made him nervous. The fool would probably see a rock that looked like a rune, get distracted, and drop the whole illusion.

"It's not a trick, my lord. I swear it!" Marcus yelped.

Mads didn't need to be a master of magic to recognize the fate of that conversation. They needed to get Terra out immediately.

They moved around a bend in the cave and found her among a pile of stolen goods that nearly made Mads blush.

Leif hurried to Terra's side, and Mads became visible

again. He glanced back up the cave, but Fenrir was still around the bend, out of sight. He ignored the piles of coins and weapons and went to Terra. He was shocked to find her unbound and told her as much.

"It's not because Fenrir's a gentleman, I can tell you," Terra whispered. "He's been draining my *seidr*. I can't hurt him in my current state."

"Not to worry. We brought the other artifacts." Leif gave her Brísingamen, and she clasped it around her neck.

"Better, luv?" Mads asked. Color had returned to her face, and she held her shoulders straighter.

"Yes, but it's still not going to be enough."

"I have the ax, too." Leif handed her that.

"It's not full," Terra noted.

"No. I'm afraid not. I used much of its energy trying to defend us against Fenrir."

"I don't want to be the bearer of bad news, but this isn't going to be enough," Terra reiterated. "He's been feeding off me and the bracers."

"What about the other artifact?" Leif asked.

"It's in here." Terra nodded at the box. Mads was shocked to see Fenrir had left it within Terra's reach. "There's a puzzle on the back of it."

"I don't think now is the time to solve puzzles," Mads insisted. "Terra, if you don't think you can take him, maybe we need to get out of here and regroup."

"Nonsense. My plan is a good one!" Leif proclaimed distractedly. He had the box in his hands and was fiddling with little moving tiles on the back.

"What's the plan?" Terra asked.

Mads listened and could still hear Marcus prostrating

himself to Fenrir farther up the cave. "Fenrir is strong enough that he shouldn't be here."

"He escaped from demigod prison. Yes, he told me."

"Right. Well, Leif thinks if we can knock the amulet off his neck, he won't be able to hide from whichever god was supposed to be on duty."

"He also might transform into a giant wolf fueled by vengeance," Terra pointed out.

"That is definitely my least favorite part of the plan," Mads confirmed. "Leif's not sure how long it would take for the gods to notice Fenrir. Considering you're not feeling your fittest, we can assume however long we last won't be enough."

"Let's get out of here, then. I can use Brísingamen to—"

A loud *click* interrupted the conversation. It echoed through the cave, a mechanical sound much louder than their whispers.

"You have done it!" Fenrir roared from farther up the cave.

Marcus started babbling something, but Fenrir shushed him, and he stomped deeper into the cave.

"Well, it looks like we were right about the cloak." Leif pulled out a beautiful garment made of feathers.

"You cheating crooks!" Fenrir roared when he came around the bend and saw Leif and Mads with Terra.

"I cannot believe it, master! They must have followed—"

With a casual backhand from Fenrir, Marcus smashed into a pile of old weapons and helmets. The crashing metal echoed and reverberated through the cave.

Mads did not fail to notice dirt falling from some of the

higher places, dislodged by nothing more than the noise. This was not a good place to have a brawl.

Terra seemed to agree. Rather than gripping the ax and bracing herself to meet the approaching wolf in man's clothing, she grabbed the feathered cloak.

"Freya's cloak has more power than I realized!" she cried. "You'll never take it!"

Fenrir growled and increased his speed.

"Get behind me," Terra told Mads and Leif.

"I'd rather get out of here," Mads insisted.

"Not without that amulet."

Terra waved the cloak, and Fenrir struck.

CHAPTER NINETEEN

A cave on the North Coast, Gotland, Sweden, Thursday Night

Fenrir was upon them before Leif could decide what illusion to use to help them. Terra held up his great-grandmother's cloak, and Fenrir charged toward it. Leif did not see how that would stop him. The dwarves had crafted a special chain merely to stop the wolf. This cloak had no such attributes.

Terra had to know this as well as Leif. She studied Norse mythology, as they called the histories on this planet, and she had asked him to fill in the pieces she did not understand. Freya's cloak did not give anyone protection. It was a thing of flight. Of transport.

Then Leif felt it. The flow of *seidr* washed out from the cloak and wrapped around him, Mads, and Terra.

And Leif felt himself *change.*

It was similar to the ring, though stranger since he was not in control. One moment, he was a man, albeit not a mortal one, preparing for his own demise. The next, he was a falcon.

He pumped his wings without thinking. Being in this body granted him the knowledge of how to use it. He lifted off the floor of the cave before Fenrir smashed into the cloak. A tiny flick of his neck revealed Mads and Terra were also birds now. Falcons.

Fenrir had yet to notice. He tackled the cloak to the ground, obviously assuming Terra was still inside.

He bit it and shook the cloak back and forth. Leif's heart stopped when several feathers shook loose, though when Fenrir finally stopped and realized his targets were gone, the cloak was undamaged. The freed feathers were caught in a wind that had not existed a few moments ago and blown into nothingness. The beautiful little illusion made Leif think of his grandmother. It was the kind of thing she loved.

Fenrir was less impressed.

Apparently remembering he was a human, not a wolf, he grabbed the cloak with his hands, pulling at it and trying to tear it to pieces. It let him. Fistfuls of feathers puffed and floated to be blown away by the same strange wind.

It was comical seeing this big, tough man lose his marbles over some feathers.

He pulled himself together, dragged the cloak to his face, and breathed in deeply. Leif could sense the cloak's magic flowing into Fenrir. Not good. He had gained enough elevation to dive and try to take the cloak from Fenrir's disgusting mitts when another falcon plunged at the back of the man's neck.

Leif smiled. Leave it to Terra to jump right into things.

She managed to grab the amulet in a talon, but Fenrir was too keyed in to the necklace to let this go unnoticed. He struck behind him. Terra pumped her wings and flew above the blow, but she had to release the amulet. It was a good thing she was a bird. If she had simply been invisible, Fenrir would have clobbered her.

The wolf in man's form might not be the brightest, but Leif still felt certain he would figure out what had happened to the three of them. Which meant Leif would only have the element of surprise a moment longer. He set his falcon eyes on the chain around Fenrir's neck, then tucked his wings and dove.

The wind whipped past as his wings made tiny adjustments to bring him closer and closer. He thought *grab* and felt his talons extend. They did not feel like feet to him any more than his wings felt like arms. They simply felt like an extension of his existence, the part of him that would do the grabbing when grabbing needed doing.

Before he could make contact, Fenrir snarled and swung at him. His falcon's wings made it easy to dodge and fly back out of reach.

However, the element of surprise was gone.

Now, three little birds would have to take from a hungry wolf.

Fenrir's hoard, Gotland, Sweden, Thursday Night

Marcus had been concerned that Leif and Mads might have overheard him agreeing to chop off Terra's hands and not understood that it was a deception. Clearly, he didn't have to worry. The three of them had transformed into birds and were taking turns dive-bombing Fenrir, trying to snatch the amulet from his neck.

The mighty wolf was used to facing Asgardian warriors. They fought directly, relying on their strength more than anything else. This was a different fight, and Fenrir seemed annoyed. It certainly did not appear that he knew how to stop the birds, nor were they skilled enough in this form to take the amulet from him yet.

Marcus was keenly aware he could probably shift the balance in this fight. He could approach Fenrir, pretending to fight the birds, and get close enough to remove the amulet. He wouldn't dare do such a thing, of course. A single blow from Fenrir would cave his ribs in, and he would rather keep them where they were for now.

He could also throw something at the birds and give Fenrir a moment against a pair of them instead of all three. Any of these actions might shift the battle one way or the other.

Marcus would not risk any of them. If he attempted a gambit for the team that *lost*, he would not live out his days. He was thinking about his future a lot these days, namely how he didn't want to have one without the shapeshifting ring.

He supposed this should make him ally with Terra and her crew. As long as Fenrir was on Earth, there would be no escaping him, but Marcus still neglected to help. What was the point of using the ring safely if he did not even have the ring?

So rather than push the scales one way or the other,

Marcus did what made sense to him. He ransacked Fenrir's piles of junk, looking for it.

He dug through coins, crowns, daggers, and hatchets. He discarded amulets, chains, and arrowheads. The thief in him felt compelled to pocket a few coins, and he did, but most of it, he simply moved past. Was this what it felt like to mature? To finally grow up?

Marcus had been wrapped up in his own survival for so long that he'd almost forgotten a human being could concern themselves with something besides gathering the resources one needed to survive. He wanted money to survive, and the ring was a means to that end, but it was also more than that. It was the single most exciting thing that had ever happened to him. Becoming a fly, a massive serpent, or gods of the north knew what else was exciting. He didn't want to give that up for enough treasure to last until the next heist.

So he tossed relics he couldn't hold and skipped over necklaces and weapons he probably could have sold to the right person for tens of thousands.

Yet he couldn't find it. It wasn't on top of anything, and no matter how much he dug around, he could not find it buried, either.

He glanced at Fenrir, and just in time, too. The wolf landed a strike on one of the falcons. The bird spiked to the ground, bounced once, then smashed into the cloak and Marcus.

If it was only the bird, it probably would not have been a big deal. But it transformed back into Mads, so a full-grown man crashed into Marcus and drove them both into a pile of artifacts.

Things scattered everywhere, but Mads ignored them. He was human once more and thus reaching for his gun.

Marcus didn't care. He only wanted one thing, and it was still eluding him.

Then he saw it.

It had tumbled out of a copper urn.

The ring.

The golden ring.

Marcus put it on his finger and felt the power flow through him.

He was back.

The power he'd claimed was his again.

Now, he only had to decide what to do with it.

Fenrir's creepy cave, Gotland, Sweden, Thursday Night

Mads was glad not to be a bird anymore. All that shapeshifting, magic powers and whatnot was great, but it wasn't for him. He was a man of this Earth. Always had been and would be until the end of his days. Rather, considering his current circumstances, until the end of his seconds.

If he was going down fighting, he wanted to do so with a barrel of steel in his hands.

And he'd brought one to do the job.

When Terra transformed him into a bird, he wondered what had happened to the bag with his gun in it. Now that he was human again, he discovered he still had it on him. A neat trick, that. He'd have to thank Terra for it later. If there was a later.

He pulled out his AR-15, took aim, and waited for the

Terra and Leif falcons to get clear. Then, he fired his shot. He aimed for Fenrir's neck, figuring if he missed, he'd hit the face, chest, or, with a little luck, the amulet itself.

The sound of the gun was deafening in the cave, but that didn't bother Mads. Anything to take this bastard down. He struck true. Three bullets in Fenrir's neck and another few in his shoulder.

It didn't even slow the beast down. He only turned toward Mads with malice in his eyes.

"You dare use mortal weapons against me?" Fenrir growled.

"No, mate. I wouldn't do it again. Regretting having done it at all, I should say." That was all true, but when Fenrir stomped toward him, Mads broke his promise and shot the bastard in the face.

Fenrir roared in pain and grabbed his eyes. Scratched out the bullets like they were grains of sand. Focused on Mads.

That was his mistake. With his attention fully on Mads, it was finally possible for Terra to swoop down and snatch the amulet from Fenrir's neck.

Fenrir howled in rage and swiped at her as she flew past.

She dropped it at Mads' feet.

Not wanting to do anything else to piss off the demigod, Mads did not let himself think. He had a duty. To his friends, his boss, and hell, even this entire world. The amulet skittered to a stop, and he did what he had to.

He shot it.

Fenrir might have been strong enough to resist bullets, but this ancient piece of stone was not. It shattered with a single shot, though Mads fired a few more to be sure. Magic flowed into the air.

"No!" Fenrir gasped, diving for the amulet and landing with just enough time to pass his hands through the wisps of escaping magic. He looked at Mads with something like dread in his eyes for the first time.

Mads felt a stab of pride. They had done it. They had accomplished what they'd set out to do, not because they had stuck to a specific plan but because they trusted each other, improvised, and made it work.

That tiny bit of pride might have swelled to something more. Yet before it could, Fenrir began to change.

He was already on all fours, so when he stuck his head out, the way his head snapped back almost looked normal. Then his neck thickened, and his jaws extended past his lips. His tongue lolled out, and his ears shot up, tufts of fur on their triangular tips.

His jacket tore next, revealing rippling muscles with black fur growing over them. The sound of grinding bone as his shoulders shifted to become front legs instead of a human's prehensile limbs. His hips sounded like they shattered and rebuilt. His pants shredded as his legs changed and bent in different places.

His fingers did not so much shrink as the meat of his hands grew between them. A tail extended from his rigid spine. He arched his back and howled so loudly that a chunk of rock fell from the ceiling and crashed to the ground.

He was a wolf now. And he was growing. At first, he was simply the biggest wolf Mads had ever seen. Bigger than a man, big as a bear, but that was already a thing of the past. Fenrir howled again as muscle layered on top of muscle. His bones extended, making him a wolf as large as a horse. It wasn't as simple as that, though. The front half of his body was bulky. Mads had a feeling his front paws would have tremendous power. However, it was the mouth that struck fear in his heart.

His teeth were jagged and all different lengths, like he enjoyed chewing on bone, steel, and anything else he could find. His jaw muscles were so substantial it looked like he could crush Mads in one bite.

Suddenly, their plan to break Fenrir's amulet and try to fight him long enough for reinforcements seemed poorly thought out.

CHAPTER TWENTY

Fenrir's hoard, Gotland, Sweden, Thursday Night

Marcus would not say he was underwhelmed by Fenrir's transformation. Maybe he was expecting more. Fenrir had become the largest wolf Marcus had ever seen, yet he was still undeniably a wolf. A wolf with a barrel chest and teeth like knives, but a wolf all the same.

He would not disparage the man who had so mercilessly cajoled him in his human form. However, now that he saw the extent of what the amulet had been hiding, it seemed maybe he had overreacted. It was a large wolf, but Marcus could become an even larger snake. It might be difficult to fight a demigod, but if Marcus threw in with Terra, Mads, and Leif, they could prevail.

Any thought of helping evaporated when Fenrir pointed his snout full of jagged teeth at Marcus.

"Betrayer," he snarled, his voice more guttural than it had been as a man.

"No, sir! I would never. I was forced. I didn't want to. They *made me do it!*"

Fenrir lunged and flew. Without fully realizing what he was doing, Marcus took the form of a snake. He moved his sinuous neck out of the path of the wolf's teeth and instead let him bite him at his thickest point. It hurt, but Marcus knew he could shift out of the grip. Fenrir tried to shake him like a ragdoll, but Marcus was too massive as a serpent. He struck Fenrir in the back of the neck once, twice, three times, pumping venom into the wounds.

Fenrir, the stupid beast, should have released him and backed away. Instead, he tried to bite down harder on Marcus, but he couldn't. His mouth was hardly wide enough to reach around his middle, let alone apply the pressure to crush him.

At least, that was how it seemed when Fenrir had first bit Marcus. Yet suddenly, Marcus' body fit inside the wolf's mouth just fine. Suddenly, his teeth were slicing into Marcus' flesh, digging through meat and trying to crush bone. Marcus threw coils around the wolf, but he couldn't wrap him up like he should have been able to do.

He shifted from a massive snake to a tiny rat. He had practiced enough with the ring that he could control how he shifted, so he made his entire body shrink into his head. Only a rat's tail had to slip from Fenrir's jaws.

Fenrir roared as his prey escaped. Marcus ran into a helmet and quivered.

"Come out, Marcus," Fenrir roared, but Marcus did no such thing. He stayed where he was and peeked out at the huge wolf. There had been a time when being small skewed his perceptions of scale, but with his experience taking different shapes, he had learned to put anything in human terms. And in human terms, Fenrir had grown.

He was no longer simply the size of a horse. Now, the wolf was as big as a truck and still growing. Fenrir inhaled with his massive snout. His wet nose quivered, then he looked directly at Marcus.

Marcus ducked back inside the helmet. From this angle, he saw the other three had taken their human shapes again. The cowards weren't even going to stay and fight!

Fenrir stomped toward Marcus, and he yelped in fear. He was too scared to move. The helmet filled with the smell of rat urine. Then Fenrir was there, gobbling the entire pile of ancient metal like it was dog kibble.

Marcus jumped from the helmet before he became the juicy center of a treat, then turned into a fly in midair. Fenrir snapped his huge jaws, but Marcus slipped through his teeth and made for the exit.

"Marcus, no! We can't let him get to the surface!" Terra shouted as Marcus buzzed by. He was going to ignore her. But to his absolute shock, she moved deeper into the cave, ready to square off against the huge wolf with nothing but a hand ax, a necklace, and some bracers.

Marcus could not fathom why anyone would do such a thing. Was it because she had the ability to teleport? Did she think she could escape? If she intended to use her teleportation to get away, why go closer to the wolf? It would have been simpler to vanish and let the wolf gobble up the men working with her. That was what Marcus would have done.

And that was why Marcus was alone.

Terra was not abandoning them because she was their friend. Perhaps more than that, she was thinking about others, not only herself. She was thinking about the whole of Gotland, maybe beyond.

Marcus still thought she was an idiot, soon to be a dead idiot, but he settled in near the lip of the cave to watch. It wasn't that he thought she could win. She probably knew she *couldn't* win, yet she was still trying. He didn't think of Terra as a hero, but she was acting like one. It was closer to heroic than anything Marcus had seen.

Fenrir's cave, Gotland, Sweden, Thursday Night

Terra couldn't let Fenrir get out of this cave. She was exhausted and out of magic, but she had to keep him here. He was a demigod too dangerous to be let loose on Asgard. If he got past her, the entire island of Gotland could be dead before dawn. He had already doubled in size, and he didn't show any sign of slowing.

So she got right to it.

She marched into the cave, ax in hand, feeling empty. No. Not empty. That was the wrong way to think about it. The ax was thirsty. Thirst for a taste of magic from the giant wolf.

Fenrir surged up from the depths of the cave. Terra stood in his way, then she ran toward him. The wolf swiped a paw at her, and she jumped over it. The paw alone was bigger than a regular wolf. Not good odds, Terra had to admit. She landed on the ground and swung her ax at the huge wolf's chin.

She connected. When the blade struck, Terra did not focus on sending her power *into* the wolf but on taking it from him. She couldn't overpower him in her current state.

Hell, she might *never* be able to overpower him, so she didn't try. The ax had nicked the underside of the wolf's chin. Through that wound, Terra siphoned energy back to herself.

Fenrir tried to eat her, but she had enough power to teleport away. She reappeared thirty feet back, closer to the entrance of the cave. She had been low on power and didn't have a great sense of the cave, so she appeared a few feet above the ground and fell. Got to her feet, readied herself for another attack.

It didn't come. Not at first. Fenrir roared as blood dripped from his chin. Then, from the wound, more hair sprouted. Longer, thicker hair. His neck surged with more muscle, then his shoulders and chest broadened. Without the amulet, he was using his own magic to keep his size in check.

A plan formed in Terra's head. Not a great one. A bad one, really, but what choice did she have?

She ran back toward the wolf. Fenrir snapped at her, but she dodged past him and got underneath him, then sliced his belly with her ax. Again, she focused on siphoning magic from the wolf into herself. She felt herself invigorated by the return of the power he'd taken. It didn't make Fenrir weaker.

However, she had beaten one foe by letting him overpower himself. She could do it again.

The wounds on his belly healed in an instant. More muscle formed, and his ribs seemed to expand to support the growth. Then he was even larger.

Too big to get out of the cave, in fact. Now for the riskiest part of the plan.

Terra teleported to the entrance, beside where Marcus sat as a fly.

Before he could buzz away, she grabbed him in her hand. He bit her immediately. His venom made the wound sting, but Terra didn't let go.

"Marcus, I know you've always been a cowardly piece of crap, but you don't have to be."

The fly buzzed, but she did not release it.

"This bastard has been hurting you, controlling you, making you waste a treasure you've learned how to use. Now, you can put an end to him. All you need to do is fly down there, bite him on the face, then fly deeper into the cave. He'll chase you. I'll hit him again, and he'll grow too big to escape. We'll have him trapped, and we'll have you to thank. But you have to do it *now*."

Now, for the leap of faith. Terra opened her hand and let the fly go.

He buzzed around the entrance, briefly dipping into the freedom of the night before returning to the cave.

"I'll put in a word with our boss, and we'll get you a nice reward, mate! Tax-free and a fake passport to boot!" Mads called.

The fly buzzed directly at the massive wolf's face.

He bit him on the eyelid. Terra could hardly see the fly, but she saw the bright red blood spill from the wolf's brow into his eye. As she suspected, the wolf immediately forgot about Terra. Now, all he wanted was to kill the insolent speck causing him so much pain.

He snapped at the fly, snapped again, then turned his massive body to follow the fly deeper into the cave. Marcus might not deserve it, but Terra would honor her word. She ran toward them, chasing Fenrir deeper. The walls of the cave shook when Fenrir brushed them. He didn't reach the cavern ceiling yet, but it seemed only a matter of time before he did.

Terra would not give him that time.

She ran up behind him. His tail, the size of an entire person, came down near her, and she swung her ax at its base.

She had barely enough strength to slice through the tail. Magic flowed from the wound, and she sucked it up with the ax.

Then the tail started to regrow, and she got the hell out of there.

Fenrir had forgotten about the fly and was trying to get to Terra again. Yet severing his tail had made him lose control of his magic. He was growing larger. Muscles rippled from the wound. The sound of his bones grinding echoed through the cave.

The walls shook as Fenrir tried to turn around, but there wasn't enough room. He might be a demigod of great strength, but rock was rock. It would not give way to make room for a grumpy beast, no matter how large.

Terra raced to the entrance as the wolf tried and failed to move out of the cave.

Fenrir howled in rage. Then the cave roof fell in, and the mighty wolf was buried under the earth.

CHAPTER TWENTY-ONE

North shore, Gotland, Sweden, Early Friday morning

Terra stepped from the cave and peered back inside. She waited for Marcus to come out. Surely, he would not have wanted to stay down there, but no fly or bat emerged from the cave. Nothing emerged except dust and the ever more distant cries of Fenrir as he brought more rocks and earth down on top of him.

After a moment, even the rumbling of his struggles stopped.

"I never thought that would work," Terra panted.

"Trapping him in the cave?" Leif asked.

"Getting Marcus to lure him deeper," Terra replied.

Mads snorted. "You never can tell with thieves. We're brave as anything when we're not being cowards."

"Brave? Is that right? I can't say I've seen any evidence of that with you," Leif retorted.

"Well, that's because I'm not a thief, you cheeky bugger. I work with a team of archeologists trying to stop ancient magical weapons from being wielded against the population. A proper hero I am, not that you'd know it from the way you lot treat me."

"I didn't know a hero cared about how others treated him," Leif replied.

"Well, of course you wouldn't know. You're about as far from a hero as possible."

"You're both heroes," Terra insisted. "I was trapped in there, and you two came to my rescue."

"Only because we knew you're the best with the artifacts," Mads stated and patted her on the back.

Terra turned to the east and saw the sun starting to illuminate the edge of the ocean. A storm brewed way out there, but a few stars remained overhead. It was peaceful.

For about a minute.

Then, the ground beyond the mouth of the cave heaved up and collapsed.

Terra, Mads, and Leif all cursed in their language of choice. A bat shot from the collapsed ground. It seemed Marcus had used up all his bravery.

Terra wasn't sure how much more she had left, either.

From the hole, a mountain seemed to rise. It wasn't a mountain but the shaggy back of Fenrir. A huge paw reached from the wreckage and stepped on the ground in front of them. To say it was as big as a tree was an understatement. It was massively thick and covered in coarse hair. Each claw was as big as a rhino's horn. When another foot emerged from the hole next to it, it felt as if a forest was growing before their eyes.

When Fenrir's head burst from the hole and rose above the pair of legs, it felt like a volcano was erupting.

Fenrir howled, and the ground shook.

"That's more what I was thinking," Mads remarked, running a hand through his hair.

"He can't escape notice in this form," Leif announced.

"We have to keep him from heading toward any of the population," Terra insisted.

"A noble plan," Leif agreed.

"I'm assuming if I suck away enough of his magic, he'll collapse?" Terra wondered.

"What makes you assume that?" Mads question.

"I need to assume something besides that I'm about to get eaten," she returned.

"Drain his magic, yes!" Leif shouted.

"*I hunger!*" Fenrir howled.

Terra figured the time for talking with him was gone.

Fenrir lowered his massive snout to look at them.

"Don't be rude!" Terra shouted, then slashed his nose with her ax. A bright red gash opened, and she drew energy from Fenrir back into her. Not as much as she would like, but it was a start.

Then, it was Fenrir's turn. He snapped at Terra, and she teleported out of the way, a hundred feet back. It felt like she was still directly in front of the damn wolf. He looked even bigger when seen from afar, which hardly seemed possible and definitely seemed unfair.

Lacking teleportation abilities, Leif blasted Fenrir in his massive eye with a glowing orb of energy. Like all Leif's blasts, it lacked power, but the bright light was not welcome. Fenrir howled and swiped clumsily at Leif, who dodged out of the way.

"Not sure how I'm supposed to help with this one!"

Mads ran to his car. He didn't get in the front but opened the trunk. Going for more weapons.

Terra couldn't let the thief one-up her. She teleported back into the battle, but this time, she appeared well above Fenrir. She fell through the air, the wind snatching at her clothes as she approached the wolf's back. When she landed, she grabbed his fur with her free hand and planted her feet on his back.

Fenrir did not seem to notice an entire human landing on his back.

Leif was still trying to dodge snaps from the massive jaws. Fenrir was still trying to eat him.

Terra would change that. She wrapped a tuft of fur around her hand, then swung the ax down with all her might. She sliced through skin and meat, then felt the ax thud into bone.

Fenrir felt it, too. He howled in pain and shook his coat like a dog trying to dry off after falling into the pool. The bracers greatly enhanced Terra's strength, so she managed to hold on for almost six seconds.

But the force of an avalanche overwhelmed even the most stalwart of creatures living on a mountain. Terra felt the fur rip from her hands, then she was careening through the air, high above the huge wolf and her friends he was trying to eat.

The sun appeared a tiny bit higher, though maybe that was Terra's extreme vertical position in the sky. She reached the top of her arc and started to fall back down. Rather than let gravity run its course and smash her into the ground, she teleported out to the sea and splashed into the cold water of the Baltic.

She wondered if Leif would chide her later for falling into yet another body of water. He certainly wouldn't if he was eaten by a wolf.

Terra surfaced and teleported back to dry land, near the fight. She had taken enough *seidr* from Fenrir to access all her abilities again. Being in that fur made her think of only one thing. Fireball.

She started a spark in her hand and grew it. First to the size of a baseball, then a watermelon, then bigger than herself. When she'd used up nearly all the *seidr* she'd taken back, she hurled the fireball at the mighty wolf.

He sensed it coming, no doubt from the magic, and turned to face it. Yet he was sluggish and unable to fully brace for the blow. The fireball caught the wolf in the armpit, and he fell.

Fenrir toppled backward and landed on top of the cliff that led down to the beach. He kicked and tried to right himself, but the stone of Gotland was no match for the celestial force of nature that was a pissed-off Fenrir.

His thrashing turned the cliffs into rubble.

Terra braced herself, creating a barrier of protection with the bracers as stone and rubble fell around her. Fenrir smashed onto the beach and kicked his huge legs in the air. He looked like a dog rolling in the world's biggest piece of roadkill. Terra wondered if he thought she was still on his back. Probably not. He seemed beyond thought. A beast of pure instinct and rage.

And Terra had thrown a fireball at him.

She dropped her barrier and started toward him. She would meet him in the shallows of the Baltic Sea and do battle. If she died here, hopefully, Freya would grant her a spot in Folkvangr. One could dream, she supposed.

She wouldn't go willingly, though.

While Fenrir struggled and finally regained his feet, Terra ran across the beach with her ax in hand.

Fenrir lunged, but his massive size made him easy to predict. He was going to try to eat her. Terra jumped above his jaws, landed between his eyes, and swiped at an eyeball with her ax.

Fenrir was able to lift his head. In doing so, he sent her flying for the second time.

She reached for her power, but there wasn't enough to teleport. So she careened through the air, and like a biscuit-obsessed dog, Fenrir tracked her with gaping jaws. She would have fallen down his throat. That would have been the end of it had Mads not chosen that moment to open fire on the big wolf.

Gunshots rang out, and Fenrir flinched from the wounds. Terra didn't see any blood, but her position from above was hardly a good one. She focused on landing on his back. Again, she crashed down and managed to grab Fenrir's fur. She briefly got a glimpse of Mads and Leif on what was left of the cliff.

Fenrir saw them, too. Which meant Terra had to act. She hacked into his fur and tried to drain more *seidr*. She felt herself replenished, but not as much as before. She realized both of them were using the same supply of magic at this point. Fenrir no longer had a tether to any other realm, and he'd been siphoning away what power Terra had. She was taking it back, but both of them were expending it.

She figured in a battle of attrition, she would win. After all, she was from this world, while Fenrir was not. However, this was not a battle of attrition. Fenrir might run out of power, but he still had more than enough strength to snap her in half.

This time, she tried to hold onto his fur as he attempted to shake her free. She kept her grip, so Fenrir rolled onto his back. Terra hit the sand and scrambled away, trying to escape the huge bulk of the wolf coming down on top of her. The only consolation was that if Fenrir ate her corpse, he'd get a mouthful of dog hair and sand. The worst of all textures.

Her friends would not give up on her, though. More gunshots from above, and Terra scrambled clear of Fenrir as he scratched at the cliff. Mads and Leif jumped back, but not enough to escape the landslide Fenrir created. They slid down with it.

Now, all three were on the beach with Fenrir.

They could not escape. Could not go for more weapons. This was it.

Fenrir knew it. He shook himself, and sand and dirt flew from his coat. It caught the light of the morning sun. For a moment, it looked like they were battling a cloud with teeth and haunting yellow eyes. Then, the dust and dirt cleared, and they once again faced Fenrir.

"You are weak," the mighty wolf panted.

"And you're tired," Terra returned.

The wolf licked his chops and pulled his tongue back into his mouth, but it lolled right back out.

"Why fight us when it's Loki you want?" Terra shouted, desperate to buy them more time.

It was the wrong tactic. Fenrir howled the name of his father, and the entire island of Gotland shook with his fury.

Leif and Mads knew what to do. One shot darts of light, and the other a storm of bullets. Fenrir closed his eyes to protect himself and lunged forward. With his size, he didn't even need to aim. He only had to crush them.

Terra wouldn't let him, though. She sprinted forward and to the side, barely missed a leg, then turned to slice it. Magic flowed into her, but it wasn't enough. They were both running out of power. It would be a stalemate, which meant Fenrir would continue to exist on Midgard. Terra had to count that as a loss.

She had enough power to teleport, so she took to the air and landed on his face.

However, she misjudged how tall the wolf was and appeared directly in front of his massive yellow eye. He whipped his jaws toward her and opened wide. Clamped them down on Terra.

She created a barrier around herself to prevent being crushed. She pushed up, trying to resist the power of the wolf's mouth. She stood on his tongue. His jagged teeth were all around her. It smelled worse than any doggy breath from Midgard. Fenrir squeezed, closing his jaws, and trying to crush her.

Then, distantly, she heard a crack of thunder. Her entire world shifted as she was knocked out of Fenrir's mouth—and the demigod hurtled out to sea.

Terra barely had the wherewithal to land on the beach without breaking anything.

She looked up to see the thunderstorm on the horizon

had reached them. It was split in two, and at its center was a hammered bronze, elaborately decorated, floating chariot. A pair of burly flying goats pulled the conveyance, stamping at the clouds, coming to a rest after swooping down to the beach. Standing in the chariot, one hand on the reins and the other holding a hammer with a massive head and a curiously short shaft, was a man with long, flowing hair, burly shoulders, and a grin that lit up the sky.

"Finally found you, cur!" He boomed and laughed. A jolly, rollicking sound.

"I cannot believe it," Leif murmured. "They sent Thor."

CHAPTER TWENTY-TWO

The North Shore, Gotland, Sweden, Friday, dawn

Fenrir howled from the Baltic Sea.

"Such disrespect! Has no one taught you not to eat the Chosen?" Thor boomed.

"What about arrogant gods?" Fenrir growled, planting his feet on the sand beneath the sea, readying himself to pounce.

"If I see any, I'll let you know." Thor winked at Terra.

"Oh, my gods. You think he's going to change, but he never does," Leif muttered.

Fenrir had already had enough of the god of thunder. He lunged, and when he did, Terra thought her entire understanding of gravity might have been completely misguided.

It should not have been possible for something that large to leave the Earth. Even the sea rebelled at the idea of it. When Fenrir leaped out to bite Thor from the air, the shoreline receded to fill the void the massive wolf had created.

The wolf opened his massive jaws. Terra had been in his mouth a moment ago. She knew how big it was. Fenrir could not swallow a chariot, two goats, and the god of thunder in one bite. Except now it looked like he could. His jaws opened wider and wider, like a snake.

"Grinder, Gaptooth, mind the wolf!"

The goats kicked at the clouds, and the chariot sprung into motion, shooting upward and above the wolf leaping from the sea. Thor held tight to the reins, his muscles bulging as the chariot flipped up behind the goats. Despite the goats using the clouds themselves to maneuver, it looked like it might not be enough. Fenrir's gaping mouth was huge.

With Fenrir's mouth poised to swallow the chariot, Thor bopped him on the nose with his hammer. There came a crack of thunder from Mjolnir as it collided with Fenrir's snout, and the wolf slammed back into the ocean.

"Brace yourselves!" Leif shouted as a mighty tidal wave rose.

Mads grabbed one of Terra's arms, and Leif grabbed the other.

Terra thought they were crazy until she looked at the collapsed wall of scree behind them. No trees remained standing, thanks to Fenrir. The boulders and stone were scattered. There was no way to know which of them, if any, would survive the force of the wave.

So Terra pulled on what *seidr* she had and sunk her feet into the beach. She imagined herself staying here, anchored to the shore, as the water washed over them. Her fate would not end by sputtering and thrashing out to sea. There was more to her tale.

The wave roared over them, and Terra felt her thighs and core flex in resistance to the pull of the water. Leif and Mads' feet were knocked out from under them, but they clung to her arms like barnacles as the water washed in, reached the scree of the collapsed cliff, then washed back out.

Somehow, none of the boulders or rocks struck them as the force of the wave sucked them out to sea. Part of Terra understood this was her power at work. *Seidr* was more than smashing and crashing, fireballs, and blasts of power. Still, it felt like a miracle when they could breathe again and had not been clobbered by any boulders.

"Looks like you've worked him into quite the lather," Thor announced, his goats descending to land his chariot not far from the soaked trio.

"I didn't mean to," Terra told him. She had met the beautiful Freya, but that had not been much of a shock since she used her power as her own. She had met wise Odin, who offered eternal life after death to Leif. Easy enough to say no to.

Yet meeting Thor, young and virile in appearance, with rippling shoulders and a smile that could stop clouds from dropping rain, was entirely different. Unlike Freya and Odin, who asked for her service and her friend's life, Thor didn't seem to be asking for anything.

"It's quite all right. I shouldn't have taken that nap. I wouldn't have if that soup from Hel wasn't so delicious!"

Behind him, Fenrir was bracing himself against the rush of water he had created when he crashed into the sea. Thor was so unconcerned that he didn't even watch to see if the wolf was attacking him yet.

"You accepted a meal from Hel when her brother was roaming free on her plane of existence?" Leif asked. Terra half expected a bolt of lightning to strike him for the impertinence, but Thor hardly seemed to notice.

"It would have been rude to say no! It gave me terrible indigestion, so naturally, I slept it off."

"Fenrir escaped because you were *napping* during guard duty?" Leif sputtered.

"The clever cur knew he couldn't slip past me while I was awake." Thor grinned like he had planned this entire thing. "He's smarter than he looks, though not as strong. You two be careful, now. Daddy's going to finish this one on his own. It wouldn't do to get stuck here."

Grinder stopped the relentless movement of his jaw to bleat affectionately while Gaptooth only stared blankly at Thor. It was quite obvious which of the goats was which.

"Might we perhaps get a ride away from this battle, your god of thunder-ness?" Mads asked, bowing his head to Thor.

"Oh, sure. Grinder, these three can have a ride to the top. I'll finish up with this pup."

The water had stopped rushing past Fenrir, and the mighty wolf took a step forward, then another.

Terra, Leif, and Mads did not need to be told twice. They clambered into the elaborate chariot and held on tight.

"Pip, pip, you two," Thor called, and the goats stepped into the air, climbing a mountain path that was not there until they reached the section of cliff Fenrir had not reduced to rubble.

Just in time, too.

Fenrir charged from the sea, creating a massive wake as he beelined for Thor.

Thor cracked him across the jaw and sent the huge wolf somersaulting backward, but Fenrir understood the stakes now. If he lost this battle, his freedom went with it.

He touched the ground and was already charging back. Thor wound up to strike again, but his timing was off. The wolf crashed into him while his arm was still pulling back. Mjolnir flew off and landed on a boulder, crushing it.

"That can't be good," Mads gasped.

"Oh, pish. He's toying with Fenrir. It's all rather immature, really," Leif drawled.

Fenrir pinned Thor to the ground under a giant paw and squeezed.

Thor grunted under the weight of the beast. "You're stronger than I expected you to be in this realm, Fenrir." Thor's shoulders bulged as he shoved the huge paw off him, twisted behind it, then slammed the wolf's ankle to the sand.

Fenrir yelped and twisted forward, trying to prevent the bone in his leg from snapping.

His face smashed the ground, and a huge cloud of sand and spray blew into the air.

When it cleared, there was no sign of Thor. Not until Fenrir was yanked backward and tossed into the ocean again.

Thor brushed the sand and fur from his hands.

"He really is a brute, isn't he?" Thor mused as Fenrir paddled back to shore. Thor had thrown him so far that he couldn't touch bottom. "I was thinking I might take off my belt to even the playing field, but I don't think I will."

"What about your hammer?" Leif hollered down.

Thor waved the suggestion away.

"He's only doing this because you're here," Leif grumbled. "He's not one to cheat on his wife, but he certainly likes showing off to whoever he can."

"Lucky me," Terra mumbled.

Fenrir reached the shallows and bounded through the water. He was smaller now, Terra thought. *Only* the size of a monster truck. Faster, too. Terra wondered if he had intentionally changed his size or if it meant he was losing some of his power.

He came up on the shore and circled the god of thunder. He snapped, snapped again, and when Thor went for a counterpunch, Fenrir clamped his jaws around Thor's forearm.

"Oh, no. You won't do me like you did Tyr," Thor chuckled and threw a vicious elbow into Fenrir's nose. When it connected, lightning struck from the sky above, augmenting the blow and knocking Fenrir down.

The wolf thrashed and managed to kick Thor in the gut, sending him flying. Thor thudded into the cliff face, out of sight of the chariot, though they felt the reverberations from the strike.

Then Thor was racing toward the wolf again, undeterred, undiminished in power.

Fenrir arched his back and snapped at the approaching god. Thor paid him no heed. He raced into the wolf's open jaws. Fenrir tried to clamp them shut, but Thor grabbed his tongue and yanked. Fenrir gagged, and Thor released, kicked off the wolf's bottom jaw, and landed on his head. He stomped Fenrir's face into the sand again. A gust of wind caught Thor and floated him down to land in front of the injured wolf.

Terra had been watching the entire time, but Fenrir seemed smaller still. The size of a pickup truck now. It had to be intentional because it made him faster. He got up and shook, then snapped at Thor, clamping onto his bicep and making the god bleed.

Thor kicked him off, but Fenrir let go before the full force of the blow landed. He darted forward and scratched the god's chest. Thor fell backward, and Fenrir pounced, crushing him to the sand. Thor pulled his legs together and threw the wolf back, but Fenrir was on him again before Thor planted his feet.

His jaws snapped at Thor's neck, but the god of thunder managed to get an arm in between him and the jaws of the wolf. Fenrir sunk his teeth into Thor's armpit, and the god yelped in pain, then hit him with a knee. Fenrir didn't let go and only bit down harder. More blood spurted from Thor.

He screamed in pain, and dread filled Terra's heart. Was this how it looked when a god was killed? Leif said Ragnarök had happened. The gods had died. Thor's own heart had been stopped by the venom of Fenrir's brother. Were they about to witness his demise? How long would it take for him recover? Nine days? What did that mean on Midgard? Would Fenrir drink Thor's power and rule Midgard in his absence?

Thor's scream intensified, and the clouds above boiled and darkened. Thunder rumbled, and a bolt of lightning shot from the sky and tore into Fenrir. It lit the wolf's fur on fire, and still, the huge beast did not relent. Not until another lightning bolt struck, then a third, and a fourth. Finally, the wolf released Thor and loped off to extinguish his burning fur in the sea.

Thor was a bloody mess on the beach. His left side was a mass of puncture wounds and blood. He coughed, rolled over, and pushed himself up.

Fenrir turned back to him, tongue lolling.

"You should not be this strong on Midgard, pup of Loki," Thor called. "You have been taking magic from others, have you not?"

"You Aesir take what is not yours and claim it as your own. You have no right to the power you hold."

"I disagree." Thor held out his open hand. He didn't point it at Fenrir and call down more lightning, though. He was reaching out to his side. "I *am* the god of thunder. My father is Odin, who rules in Asgard by rights of the wisdom that he sacrificed his own eye to receive. He has ruled since time began and will rule until time stops."

"That was supposed to be the deal, but your kind broke it," Fenrir snapped.

"Enough talk, pup of Loki. Let's finish this. I haven't had a proper flagon of mead since you snuck out."

Fenrir could not resist Thor's childish goading. He howled and charged the god of thunder. The wolf wasn't paying attention when Mjolnir was ripped from its standing place and raced through the air, across the beach to Thor's open hand. The god of thunder caught his hammer and swung it onto the top of Fenrir's head.

Thunder cracked when it struck, and a great plume of sand shot up around Fenrir. Terra had the awesome realization that Leif was right. Thor had barely been trying.

When the sand fell back to the ground, Thor stood triumphant over an unconscious Fenrir, hardly larger than a horse.

"Grinder, Gaptooth!" Thor called, and the pair of goats pulled the chariot into motion and down a road of nothing but air.

"There should be a chain in there," Thor told them.

Mads smiled and pulled a tiny loop of silver chain from his wrist. "Sorry. Old habits and all that."

Thor threw back his head and laughed. "Loki would like you, I'm sure!" He took the tiny chain from Mads. When he moved to put it around Fenrir's neck, it was already large enough to circle his throat. Then it was longer still, long enough to bind the wolf's legs and snout. "Gleipnir improved," Thor announced.

"A wise choice, my lord. Better than having him run free," Leif mentioned.

Thor shrugged. "I suppose so. I went to the realm of the dwarfs, thinking Fenrir might have wanted vengeance. I certainly would have. When I told them he'd escaped, they made this for me. Could have offered me a drink, too, but I suppose they felt rushed."

"What happens to Fenrir now?" Leif asked.

"I'll slip him back into Niflheim. If I'm lucky, no one will have even noticed I was gone. Not many of the Aesir have been interested in Niflheim since Ragnarök. Too many harsh memories. Yet, I have to stand guard over this bad pup. Hardly fair. I don't feel the drain of being in Midgard like he does. Maybe we can have a proper match next time I'm on duty if Tyr doesn't kill him when he finds out."

"You really think the other gods have not noticed this incursion into Midgard?" Leif asked.

Again, Thor hardly seemed to register the impertinent attitude. "I would appreciate it if the Chosen of Freya does not make unnecessary noise about this, but if you feel you must, you must," Thor shrugged and grinned. "So be it! I've angered Freya before, and I'm sure I'll anger her again."

The god of thunder laughed, and the clouds above cleared, letting in the morning sun.

THE STORY CONTINUES

The Chosen By Freya story continues with book five, *Divine Storm*, available at Amazon.

Claim your copy today!

AUTHOR NOTES

DECEMBER 13, 2023

Hey there, and thanks for reading this book and this series, and sticking around to explore a bit more about me through these author notes. I'm glad we can share a moment beyond the pages of these stories.

I'm excited to chat with you about the new series that's been brewing in my mind—a fresh expansion of the Para-Military Recruiter universe that I hope will knock your socks off.

A New Beginning for an Outsider

Our protagonist, shunned by her own kind (she is a dwarf), finds herself at a pivotal crossroads. Ostracized and isolated, her world seems to crumble around her until an unexpected beacon of hope shines through the darkness. The Queen, a figure of immense power and insight, sees potential where others see pariah. She extends a hand, offering not just a new role but a new perspective on life itself as she has to learn the 'other side' and go to Earth... A bit out of her comfort zone.

The irony is not lost on our character. She, who has

faced the biting sting of judgment, realizes through her interactions with humans—the most unpredictable of races—that she, too, has harbored her own unfair prejudices.

A Journey of Self-Discovery

What unfolds is a story of transformation, not just of scenery, but of the soul. Thrust among humans, our heroine embarks on a journey that will force her to confront her biases, challenge her preconceptions, and ultimately uncover the core of her being. It's a tale of redemption, growth, and the power of unexpected alliances.

The Power of Friendship

Despite the odds, connections are forged, and friendships blossom in the unlikeliest of places. Our heroine discovers that those she protects offer her more than just a sense of purpose—they provide her with a mirror that reflects her true self, sometimes flawed but always striving to improve.

Excitement for What's to Come

I'm thrilled with the direction this new series is taking. It's shaping up to be a wild ride, filled with depth, action, and the kind of character development I live for as a creator. If you enjoyed The Para-Military Recruiter series, hold on to your hats because you're in for an even more exhilarating adventure.

Two for Two?

As I delve further into this universe, I feel like I've hit a sweet spot with creating fun with these Urban Fantasy stories. Unlike this series, based more on mythology coming to life, the other is based on two dimensions where we have those in both able to move between them.

Some of their history is our mythology (Arthur - Mordred...Elves, Dwarves, Trolls...)

With two potentially fantastic series weaving through this intricate world, I'm batting a thousand (in my completely and totally humble opinion)... So humble.

So, get ready because things are about to ROCK. If you haven't checked out The Para-Military Recruiter series yet (My Book), now's the time. You'll want to be all caught up before this new series hits the shelves.

Thank you, as always, for your incredible support, and here's to new beginnings and the endless possibilities they bring!

Ad Aeternitatem,

Michael Anderle

P.S. Don't forget to leave a review if you've enjoyed the journey so far, and stay tuned for updates and behind-the-scenes looks at this new series by subscribing to the MORE STORIES with Michael newsletter HERE: https://michael.beehiiv.com/

CONNECT WITH THE AUTHOR

Connect with Michael Anderle

Website: http://lmbpn.com

Email List: https://michael.beehiiv.com/

https://www.facebook.com/LMBPNPublishing

https://twitter.com/MichaelAnderle

https://www.instagram.com/lmbpn_publishing/

https://www.bookbub.com/authors/michael-anderle

BOOKS BY MICHAEL ANDERLE

Sign up for the LMBPN email list to be notified of new releases and special deals!

https://lmbpn.com/email/

For a complete list of books by Michael Anderle, please visit:

www.lmbpn.com/ma-books/

www.ingramcontent.com/pod-product-compliance
Lightning Source LLC
LaVergne TN
LVHW041915070526
838199LV00051BA/2629